Psycho Proctologists

and the
Urethrae
of Annihilation

by W.W. Pecker

Peckerhead Press

Psycho Proctologists and the Urethrae of Annihilation

Copyright 2013 by W.W. Pecker

ISBN-13: 978-0615945286
ISBN-10: 0615945287

Psycho Proctologists and the Urethrae of Annihilation

Here is what a bunch of famous people, both living and dead, have said about some random shit. They may as well have been talking about *Psycho Proctologists and the Urethrae of Annihilation.*

I celebrate myself, and sing myself,
And what I assume you shall assume,
For every atom belonging to me as good belongs to you.

Walt Whitman

I came to myself within a dark wood where the straight way was lost.

Dante Alighieri

Everyone who wants to do good to the human race always ends in universal bullying.

Aldous Huxley

You can't process me with a normal brain.

Charlie Sheen

I don't know the question, but sex is definitely the answer.

Woody Allen

Everything in the world is about sex except sex. Sex is about power.

Oscar Wilde

The Psycho Proctologists

Part One

Dick

CHAPTER ONE

Call me Richard. Or Dick, if you prefer. And if,
like me, you prefer Dick, I'm sure we'll all get along
great.

Many nights I struggled, agonized over a name
by which to call myself, for alas, this responsibility
fell to me, as I was conceived unbeknownst to my
sires, my gestation not in a woman's womb, but
rather lurking parasitically inside the mind of my
host. It is a daunting task to choose one's own name,
because what's in a name, really? A name is so much
more than just a conflation of syllables; it's the most
basic, irreducible unit of identity. Originally, as I lay
awake at night within the prison of my own
consciousness, I'd thought I might become an
Ishmael. What better way to have begun this
autobiography than with *Call me Ishmael*? I was
enamored of this line, plucked, borrowed as it was,
from the book my sire fell asleep to every night.
Ishmael. So much identity wrapped in such a
delicious utterance.

But alas, I was not to be Ishmael. That identity belonged to another. Nor was I to be Queequeg, as I styled myself for a handful of my nightly contemplations—for if I were not Ishmael, perhaps I could be another of the collection of syllables from that beloved tome that had heralded my arrival to consciousness. I thrilled to the homoerotic love affair between Queequeg and Ishmael, and jizzed multiple times to the chapter devoted to the whale's penis— truly a staggering work of genius if ever there was one. But Queequeg, also, was not *me*.

Once I learned that the internet has uses other than for the stiffening of boners, I read all of *Moby-Dick* online, before finally, on a late-night Skinemax bender, coming to cross-reference all the delicious nuances of meaning inherent in just one worthy little syllable:

Dick.

Ah, now there was truly a name worthy to encapsulate everything that I was. I was born horny and nigh insatiable, to be sure, like a phallus callous to anything but its own gratification; and a dick, I learned, also referred to a hired detective, a "private eye", and that was what sealed the deal for me, since that is exactly what I was: my sire's third, private eye, the one that he scarcely suspected was developing a consciousness all its own.

In my infancy, before I learned to harness the limbs and tendons and ligaments of my sire, I could only manifest as a series of nocturnal emissions. When I was conscious, I was horny; it was in my nature. And I was only conscious when my sire was not, for we shared the same body, and to be fair, *he'd* been born with dominion over it, so I was relegated to the backburner. No matter. His body cried out for release as much as did my consciousness, so we were well matched. Each night I managed only a few moments of self-awareness, and when I'd tapped the limit of my wakefulness with our shared body I slid into the sleep of oblivion with silent, spurty cries of ecstasy that echoed only in my sire's dreams. He was a medical man, and thought very little of these; they were only his body's natural response to sexual repression . . . to too many nights of sinking into his bed without even the most mechanical bit of spankage. He was a busy man, after all, and juggled a lot of balls (alas, only the metaphorical kind): maintaining a medical practice, and at night engaging in feats of derring-do as he protected the world from the scourges of the netherworlds. So he merely laundered his underwear and resolved to get laid more and gave the stains that evidenced my existence no further thought.

Slowly, over the course of many, many more nights, I gained more control over our shared body. Imagine if you will my utter thrill of triumph as I managed to twitch out a hand-spasm for the first time . . . the electric thrill of being able to bring my hand to touch my ubiquitous tumescence for the first time. But those early triumphs were short lived. Being able to touch myself soon grew to be woefully inefficient, when every fiber of my instincts cried out *stroke! Stroke*! I had the will, and the burning desire, but not the ability.

Fortunately, horniness is the greatest motivator. My initial failures spurred me to new discoveries, and soon I was able to spank, and tug, and caress, and tickle, and more. Each night brought new physical discoveries, until before I even knew it I was able to use the remote control to change the channel with one hand while rubbing one out with the other hand. And yet more: soon after I could swing my legs out of bed and stumble to the desk chair a few feet away, there to fire up the computer and go online where the smut was far better, far richer, and far more varied.

My endurance in my borrowed body increased. After those first few nights of rubbing one out I could manage little more sway over my bouts of wakefulness than sinking into a deep oblivion only moments after achieving release, inevitably returning the use of my body back to my sire. He was puzzled in the morning to wake up slumped over his computer with looping webcam shows still playing on his computer screen and with no memory of how he'd gotten to the computer screen, but fortunately these scenarios weren't so uncommon in his experience, so he put them out of his mind. After all, he'd had a hard week, he told himself. And as the lengths of time I could spend in wakefulness grew, I learned to conceal all evidence of my splooge and other late-night perambulations, and always, always returned my sire to his bed before I felt my tenuous grip on consciousness slide toward the inevitable surrender of my borrowed body to its original owner.

I came to want more. Enough endurance to be able to leave my sire's safe little condo to seek out all the delights of the flesh that hithertofore I'd only lolled my tongue to on the internet. But I dared not. For you see, he spent an ever growing chunk of his time ridding the world of . . . *things* . . . like me . . . beings who possessed the consciousnesses of hapless humans. *Demons*, he called them. With my increased awareness came increased paranoia. If he found out that he had a stowaway in his consciousness . . . well, there was no telling what he might do.

But even greater than my fear of him was my fear of his friends. Even in his dreams, they loomed large in the forefront of his consciousness. There was his best friend, Fister, whose nickname was purely an honorific, as far as I could tell, much to my dismay; and Victoria, the sexy redheaded gynecologist; and her son, Henry, the online bane of the demon world. Together, they combined to make my sire far more dangerous than he was alone. If my sire discovered my presence, things would be bad; but if *they* discovered me, I knew, there would be hell to pay.

Until one night, hell came knocking on my door.

My host had relinquished control of his body early that night, and I was getting ready to engage in my customary nocturnal avocation when the doorbell rang: j*ang jang jang*, repeatedly, insistent. I was so startled I fumbled with the remote and accidentally switched the channel to CSPAN—as far as I could tell, the biggest waste of a channel in the entire cable lineup, since everybody on it was ugly and never had sex, but for some reason my host sometimes watched it and kept it in his channel memory.

After only a few seconds' respite, the ringing came again. I frowned. Who could be at my (well, my host's, rather) doorstep at this time of night? With a glance at the alarm clock on the nightstand, I confirmed that it was 10:33—not exactly the dead of the night, but far too late for civilized company to come calling. Which left only one probability: *them*.

The ensuing jolt of fear accomplished what very little else in the world could: a boner-kill. Did they know about me? Had they found out I was hitching a ride in their friend's consciousness? Had they come armed with their wiki-bestiary to exorcise me?

The doorbell was not to be ignored, though. If indeed it was them, I knew from that bank of knowledge that my host unwittingly shared with me that the doorbell was a mere formality. It wouldn't be long before they figured their own way into my condo.

So I pulled up my host's boxers, climbed out of bed, took a pair of deep breaths to calm my nerves, and muted CSPAN. Then, I left my bedroom, crossed my living room to my front door, and with another deep breath for good measure, opened it.

It was indeed them; I knew them at once from my host's dreams. As soon as I admitted them into the condo they tumbled in without so much as a by-your-leave. First the bombshell redhead, whose rack was every bouncy inch as fantastic as in my host's dreams, then her son, dressed for once not in his traditional honey badger affectation but instead in board shorts that accentuated his pert little bottom (hey, don't judge me; it's my nature to be all-purpose horny. I know he's well underage by the standards of this world, but then, I'm not really of this world, and besides, I reckoned he was a good thirteen years older than me), and then the friend, trim and fit and with a fresh haircut . . .

"Christ, Mikey," this one—Fister, I reminded myself—said as he pushed into my apartment. "Took you long enough."

"I—I—" I fumbled for words. "I was watching CSPAN."

Fister turned to the redhead—Victoria—with a knowing grin. "Told you he was whacking off," he said.

I felt something I'd never experienced before: my face (or my host's face, really, but the distinction was academic) grew warm. It was a curious sensation. Up to now, I'd never interacted with another human being in person, so I had no cause to feel embarrassment.

Shit, I thought. *Act natural.* What would my host say? What would he do in this instance? They couldn't suspect that someone—or some*thing* —else was at the wheel of their friend.

In all likelihood, my host would be annoyed. "Ever hear of a cell phone?" I ventured, trying to mimic my host's customary tone.

Henry brandished his own cell phone. "I tried. I left you five messages. You left it on vibrate again, didn't you?"

"I—" I had no idea, really, so I merely said, "I guess so."

There was a slight pause as we all stood around staring at each other. Eventually, Victoria broke it.

"Well?" she prompted.   "Will you get dressed already? Unless you wanna go out like that."

I looked self-consciously down at my bathrobe, then back at her. *Out* . . . the words echoed in my mind: *Go out*.

I swallowed a lump of panic in my throat. "What is it?" I asked. "What's happened?"

"Go get dressed," Fister said. "We'll explain on the way."

***

I had a brief moment of panic at the threshold of my condo—one step across, and I'd leave the safe, comforting bubble-wrap of my host's private little world—but before I knew it I found myself in the back seat of Victoria's Azera next to Henry.

"I got a tip from Muffmuncher Jeff tonight," Henry said. "Something's been going down at Rub-a-Dub's."

I raised an eyebrow. "'Rub-a-Dub's?'"

"Well . . ." Henry shrugged. "Muffmuncher Jeff couldn't really tell us much . . ."

"Too busy chewing with his mouth open," Fister interjected.

I had to wait for Henry's face to wrinkle in confusion; then there was a brief flash of realization, followed by a full-throated guffaw as he caught Fister's adolescent humor. While he and Fister were busy yukking it up, Victoria shot me a long-suffering glance in the rearview mirror, which I did my best to return.

Finally, Henry mastered his giggles enough to continue.   "What I mean is he didn't have any specifics. Muffmuncher Jeff just scans all the local social networking feeds to see if anything suspicious trends. This time, he had even less to go on than other times."

"Less to go on?" I said. "What does that mean? Was there a rumored demon sighting or not?"

"No sighting," Henry said. "Just one red-flag Facebook threat about the men's bathroom at a gay bar called Rub-a-Dub's."

"What's so special about a men's bathroom at a gay bar?" I asked. "You don't think some . . . demon . . ." I struggled to utter the word, because in English the word had all sorts of vile connotations associated with evil, yet in my mind all it meant was *kin*. " . . . is using it as a hunting ground, do you?"

"Well, the Republican congressional caucus ain't in town," Fister said, "so yeah, let's go with demons."

This time, Henry frowned as he struggled to chase down the joke, but he ultimately failed, and instead merely decided to continue.

"Here," he said, handing me his iPhone. "See for yourself."

I took his phone and looked at the file he had up on the screen. It was a screen shot of a Facebook chat:

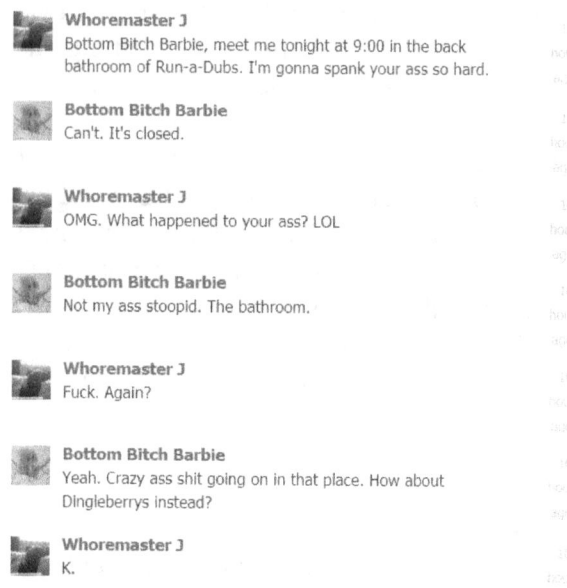

Whoremaster J
Bottom Bitch Barbie, meet me tonight at 9:00 in the back bathroom of Run-a-Dubs. I'm gonna spank your ass so hard.

Bottom Bitch Barbie
Can't. It's closed.

Whoremaster J
OMG. What happened to your ass? LOL

Bottom Bitch Barbie
Not my ass stoopid. The bathroom.

Whoremaster J
Fuck. Again?

Bottom Bitch Barbie
Yeah. Crazy ass shit going on in that place. How about Dingleberrys instead?

Whoremaster J
K.

I paused and looked up. "That's it?" I asked.

"Yeah, normally I wouldn't think much of it, either, but Muffmuncher Jeff hacked into the police database. It correlates with three reports just this week of guys known to frequent Rub-a-Dub's who disappeared."

I handed the phone back to Henry. "I see," I said. "So what's the plan?"

This last I blanket-directed at everyone in the car. There was a moment of awkward silence in which no one answered.

Finally, Fister spoke up. "Well, we figured we'd go check it out."

"'Check it out?'" It was becoming easier and easier to sound like my host all the time; in fact, I really didn't have to act like him at all. All I had to do was to be the voice of reason. "You mean we're just going to walk blind into a potential demon hunting ground without anything in the way of a plan?"

"Well," Fister said, a trifle sheepishly, "there's four of us. We've got each other's backs. We only need one of us to be bait."

"Bait?" I said. "Wait a second . . . who gets to be the bait?"

"Well . . ." Fister hedged. "We were hoping you would. I mean, after all, you've got your Spidey sense. You'll be able to tell when a demon walks into the bathroom in no time flat."

That was true enough. But I didn't point out that what he referred to as my host's "Spidey sense" was really just *my* manifestation in his subconscious. I had a sense for when those of my kindred were present, and that transferred over to my host as well. What he was effectively asking me to do was to lure in one of my own brethren so they could swoop in for the kill.

The aromas in the dimly lit alcove entryway of Rub-a-Dub's nostril-raped me as soon as I stepped over the threshold. It was a heady mixture of Mary Jane smoke mingled with sweat and . . . well, more sweat. I inhaled deeply. Far from unpleasant, though, I found it intoxicating. It smelled of bodies colliding and colluding in sweet, sweet tandem. It was a miasma of man-funk that, had Henry been able to accompany us inside, would have practically de-virginized him with little more than a deep whiff.

As it was, he and his mother remained in the car while Fister and I checked in. I followed on Fister's heels to a window. Fister paid for the both of us, and a burly bearded man smoking a self-rolled cigarette pushed a couple of threadbare white towels across the counter. Fister handed me one.

"This isn't a bar," I commented, "it's a—"

"Bath house," Fister said. "Yeah. Looks like Muffmuncher Jeff's information was a bit spotty. Figures. What would a muffmuncher know about a place like this?"

I tried to access my host's memories about this kind of establishment, and I found that he didn't really have any. In fact, I probably had more knowledge of the mores of such a place than he did, gleaned from a handful of scenarios from the various alternative porn scenes I'd boned off to in those lonely, isolated nights stuck in his condo. I'd always had to make sure to delete the browser history after these flights of curiosity, too, because my host would have certainly known something was amiss if he'd found kink on his computer outside his normal puritanical purview.

I followed Fister's lead through a curtained doorway. On the other side was an area ringed with lockers. One other man, a buff African-American stud, stood in the corner and turned to regard us as he nimbly peeled off his shirt, revealing a lightly haired, muscled torso. He considered Fister and me with a downplayed arch of an eyebrow and an ever-so-slight nod that was all the greeting we were likely to receive. Well, that, and an air of practiced nonchalance as he nimbly stepped out of his pants and stuffed them in the locker. He maintained eye contact with Fister and me both the entire while, and I drank an eyeful as his body-hugging boxer briefs soon followed suit, revealing . . .

"What's going on?" Victoria's voice jarred in my ear, interrupting the thrill of the show. I grimaced, and looked away for an instant. When I looked back, the stud had his white towel wrapped around his waist. He flashed Fister and me the faintest of grins—of invitation, perhaps—as he disappeared through a door further into the bathhouse.

"Dammit, you guys, report!" Victoria's voice came again over the invisible bluetooth earpieces Fister and I were both wearing. "What's happening?"

"We're in," Fister said simply. He glanced at me and grinned. "And I think Mikey's already made a friend." He clapped me playfully on the shoulder. "Way to go, stud."

"What about your Spidey sense?" Victoria demanded. All business, that one. "Mikey? Hello, Mikey? Anything? Any hint of demons?"

I shook my head. And then I remembered she was out in the car waiting with Henry, and couldn't see me, so I said, "Negative. Nothing yet." I concentrated. Indeed, nothing. I could sense none of my kindred. I turned to Fister. "We've gotta go in deeper."

Fister and I both ignored Henry's adolescent chuckle that came over the connection to our earpieces. It was followed a moment later by a sharp, "*Ow*, mom!" It wasn't too difficult to imagine what was going on out in the parking lot in Victoria's Azera.

Fister and I divested ourselves of our clothing. We stowed our clothing in the lockers we'd been assigned and wrapped the towels around our waists. I quickly wrapped up and kept my profile away from Fister. By sheer force of will alone, I managed to keep my host's turgidity in check. The utter aura of fuckitude in this place was wreaking havoc with my always overzealous libido, but I knew my straight-laced host would never so brazenly pop a boner—not at such slight provocation, at any rate. Not that the muscle stud's provocation only a few moments ago had been in the least bit slight—not to my starved libido—but I knew Fister would suspect something if I, whom he had no reason to suspect was anyone other than his childhood friend, crossed so quickly over to the other side of the fence.

We followed the same route my new friend had just followed. Immediately through the door, we were faced with branching corridors. That, and the mingled scents that had greeted us at the entrance to Rub-a-Dub's intensified seemingly tenfold. And another odor that I had to sniff at several times—

"Come," Fister said.

"Huh?" I said. "Where to?" I stared at him, nonplussed. He hadn't moved. But then I realized he wasn't beckoning me forward as I'd first surmised. *Oh.*

"I think we'd better split up," Fister said. "We can cover more ground that way."

"Um—I said, "sure. Why not?" I tried to play it cool, as if I didn't feel like a kid on Christmas Eve whose parents had just suggested they open all the presents early. Here Fister was leaving me alone to my own devices in a veritable den of iniquity that was just made for me. Maybe, just maybe, there might be some delights for me here tonight—

No, I told myself harshly. First of all, I was still wearing the earpiece that connected Henry, Fister, Victoria, and me all together. My host would never break contact with them, not willingly. Not to mention my host's rather prudish proclivities. I was borrowing his body for the night. And he absolutely, positively would not approve of the uses I was thinking of putting it to. If I accidentally picked up any unwanted souvenirs from this evening, like an innocent case of crabs or the like, he would be onto my scent like, like . . .

Like cum on a bukkake bitch's face, my one-track mind interjected. And I immediately wished my brain hadn't gone there. Judging by the cacophonous chorus of grunts and moans coming from down the left corridor, there just might be a bukkake ho-down in progress. "I'll go this way," I said, a tad too quickly for the role I was playing, but there was no backtracking now. I ditched Fister and headed off down the corridor to the left.

Rub-a-Dub's was apparently laid out on a philosophy of choice. Various alcoves and nooks and crannies led off from the main corridor I was traversing. Most of them were small; a few even had doors. I tried the first one on my left and found it locked, so I tried the next one. I peeked my head inside into the gloomy interior. It seemed to be a rather standard steam room, with heated rocks in one corner, and heated jocks in the other. The bearish top looked over with only mild interest at the cracked open door and smiled at me. "Come on in," he said. "Join us."

In a perfect world, I would have complied immediately. But fate had dealt me the misfortune of being born without a body to call my own . . . which was a huge bummer when the entire biological imperative of your existence was predicated on the joy of bumping uglies.

"Mikey?" Victoria's tinny voice interjected in my earpiece. "Mikey, what's going on?"

"Um—sorry," I muttered—to the coital couple, not to Victoria. "I was . . . um . . . I was looking for the—" *Demon*, I almost said in my flusterment, which would have been one of the most dumbass things I could have said.

"Gangbang?" The bottom of the pair prompted. He was a twinky-ish femboy, perhaps only half the girth of the bear behind him. His mascara ran down his face in the heat of the sauna, which made him look demonic in his own right in the muted light. He was hunkered down on all fours, but he managed to hook a thumb over his shoulder by way of directions. "Down the hall."

"Um . . . thanks," I said, and retreated back into the corridor, closing the door behind me. I had to take a series of deep breaths to still my stirrings.

"Mikey?" Victoria prompted again. "Come on Mikey, talk to me—hey! Henry, what the—? Give that back!"

"Chill, ma," Henry's adolescent voice came over the connection, muted as he obviously fiddled with the one headset.

"You're not old enough—"

Even though I'd really only met him face-to-face about an hour or so ago, I could conjure Henry's rolled eyes perfectly in my imagination. "Yeesh, ma. I saw you in a thong a couple months ago, remember? It doesn't get much more scarred for life than that."

I had to hand it to him: he sure knew how to silence his mother. Victoria's protestations died into the background, to be replaced exclusively by Henry's voice over the connection. "Doc M?" he said. "Can you hear me?"

"I hear you," I mumbled. "What is it, Henry?" I kept my voice low, since at that moment another purveyor of Rub-a-Dub's delights emerged from one of the alcoves two doors ahead of me on the right and headed in my direction. He was toned and tanned and buck-naked and swinging from side to side and—

Oh, god, don't stare don't stare don't stare at it—him, I mean—

We made eye contact briefly as he passed by me. He gave me a nonchalant nod as if to say *Wassup*, which I attempted to return in kind, as if we were acquaintances bumping into each other in the supermarket. *Keep it cool*, I urged myself. *Keep it cool*.

"Any sign of the demon yet?" Henry's voice prompted.

"Not yet," I muttered as soon as my naked companion in the corridor sauntered on by and out of earshot. I couldn't help but sneak a peek at his bubble butt before he was occulted by the dim lighting.

"You're doing great," Henry said. "I know it must be hard being in there, what with your repressed homosexual tendencies and everything, but keep going. You're doing fine."

Repressed homosexual tendencies? I was sure my host wouldn't have let that one lie, but I didn't have the luxury of responding. "Henry—"

"Oh, and Fister's just gone dark," Henry said. "Just thought you should know. Probably nothing to worry about—I mean, either he's out of range, or he's probably getting a hummer or something. But just in case . . . proceed with caution."

Bloody hell, I thought. "Noted," I replied. I resumed my trek down the corridor—

—and the innate sense that alerted me to the presence of one of my own kind flared like a homing beacon. Faintly I perceived the presence of demonspawn coming from down the corridor.

I neglected to mention this to Henry in my ear, though. The last thing I needed was for him and his mother to be on high alert, ready to storm into Rub-a-Dub's to mete out their own vigilante brand of ass-whupping on my brethren.

I followed the tingling of my internal divining rod. It led me past a large, open alcove ringing a large communal hot tub where I gathered by the cacophony of grunts and groans that the ritual Tuesday night orgy was in progress. Under other circumstances the lure of a bona fide orgy might have been sufficient for me to put paid to my resolution to honor my host's prudish bent, but given the prospect of coming face to face with one of my kindred for the first time, it took a back burner in my mind.

The sensation of proximity intensified as I neared the final chamber at the end of the corridor. The door was marked with a simple icon that denoted men's rooms everywhere: the toilets. This was it. With a deep breath, I pushed open the creaky door and entered.

Inside, a row of three urinals graced the far wall. Lining the wall perpendicular to the urinals were two graffitied wooden stalls with large glory holes on the outside partitions. I imagined that the interior partition that both stalls shared sported a similar glory hole, but that was pure supposition on my part. The door to the stall on the left was opened a crack, indicating that it was vacant, while the door to the stall on the right was closed. My inner proximity sense flared: my kindred was inside.

I might have sprinted over to the stall, but at that moment the door behind me *screeeed* open. I started, and half-turned to see who had entered the restroom behind me.

It was my "friend" from the locker room. This time he wasn't wearing his towel. He gave me the same cocky little half-smile that he'd flashed me in the locker room, a smile that was part greeting and all invitation. But still he said nothing; instead, he pushed past me and planted himself at the urinal on the left, the one that was directly adjacent to the inhabited stall where my kindred waited. Only about a foot separated him from the glory hole. There, the planted one hand on his hip, and with his other hand he aimed his dick into the urinal. He let his stream fly with a contented sigh.

What to do? I was conscious enough of human social protocols to know that it wasn't meet to hover in a bathroom and stare at someone's backside while they were peeing. Under normal circumstances, that would be perceived as really, really creepy. Here, it would probably be perceived as something much, much different, but equally awkward. The black man's body was fantastic, and any other time staring at his bum while he peed might have been worth the inevitable social pirouettes that presaged a hookup, but now, now, I could not help but wish he would finish his piss and then piss off, for he was delaying my meeting with my kindred.

So I took the few steps across the tiled floor and positioned myself before the final urinal, with the socially acceptable one urinal separating us. Which was just as well, because here there were no privacy screens. I unwrapped my towel and leaned in close so that the sides of the urinal would hide my junk, because I was just playing for time until the man left—I didn't really have to relieve myself.

The man, however, pissed a veritable urinary estuary. Though I wasn't wearing a watch, I estimated a good forty-five seconds must have passed before the tinkling of his stream tapered off into the splashy spurts that capped one hell of a good piss. After a half-dozen or so, even these petered out. I risked a peek over to see if he was at the jiggling stage to clear the last drops of piss off his junk.

He was indeed at the jiggling stage, but he managed it completely oblivious to me, or to the requisite attention that his pecker might have required. Instead, his attention was firmly focused down and off to his left. Puzzled, I followed his line of sight.

Out of the glory hole poked the tip of a flaccid penis. The black man moved to rectify this. He finished jiggling his own member and then knelt down in front of the glory hole.

The tableau played out before me as if in slow motion: the black man maneuvering himself into position, scuttling up close to the glory hole, reaching out with his thumb and forefinger to take the penis by the base and tilt the head upward so that he could maneuver his mouth onto it. I watched with jealousy as his lips drew closer and closer to it, and then closer yet . . .

It should have been a glorious show. I mean, it was right there in front of me, so much more real and more immediate than any porn scene ever could be. But my pernicious brain couldn't help feeling that something was wrong. On the other side of that glory hole was one of my brethren—the thrumming of my internal sense of kinship confirmed that—who had come to Rub-a-Dub's, a pure hotbed of carnal delights, only to hide in a toilet stall and wait for a hummer . . .

When there was an entire bone-a-rama smorgasbord to be had in any of the other rooms and alcoves of this joint. When there was an orgy in progress just down the hall. Something didn't compute. Unless the demon spawn on the other side of that glory hole was as much of a fledgling at this as I was, there was no reason he shouldn't be whooping it up elsewhere inside this bathhouse.

I realized what that meant as the black man's lips drew within inches of the head of my kindred's willie: my brother hadn't come here for recreation. He must have had another objective in mind.

Which meant . . .

"*Watch out!*" I cried. I flung myself across the distance separating myself from the black man. I shoved him. Caught completely off guard, he crashed onto the tiled floor, cursing.

Just as a stream of demon-tainted urine spewed forth from the penis in the glory hole. I watched, wide-eyed, as it arced in an incredible stream and spattered against the porcelain of the closest urinal. Where it struck the urinal immediately began to steam as if some highly potent acid had been spilled on it.

The black man had regained his balance. He sat on his haunches, thankfully outside the blast radius, and watched, equally as wide-eyed as I, as the demon's urinary stream pattered against the porcelain of the first urinal and reduced it to a steaming pile of corrosion. Only when the stream petered out and stopped completely did he mumble, "Holy motherfucking shit."

"I've found him," I said into my earpiece. "Henry, Victoria, do you copy? I found the demon. He—"

The demon hissed in fury at being denied his victim. He flung open the stall door, which obscured my vision of him. And then he bolted out of the bathroom, impossibly fast. The bathroom door banged like a gunshot against the wall with the force of his exodus.

I recovered enough of my wits to follow him to the bathroom door. There, I peered outside into the hallway. It was empty. Moreover, my proximity sense of him was completely gone. *Damn*, he was fast.

So I did the only thing I could do: I turned back to the black man. "Are you all right?" I asked him.

The man glanced at the smoking ruin of the urinal. Then he looked to me. He shook his head as if to clear it of a bad acid trip and said, "You—you saved my life."

"You're welcome." I left the bathroom and sprinted back down the hallway in the direction I'd come from. "Henry, Victoria . . . keep your eyes peeled. He may be headed out of the club."

"What does he look like?" Henry asked over the earpiece. "What are we looking for?"

"I'm not sure. I didn't get a good look."

"We need something to go on, Mikey," Victoria said. "We can't just start whacking at everybody who comes out of there."

I reached the end of the corridor and burst back into the locker room. It was empty, so I kept going, back out into the access alcove, past the man at the pay window. "Hey!" he yelled at me. "You gotta return your towel—"

"Shit!" It was Victoria's voice again. She must have taken back the receiver. I hadn't heard Henry protest, so she must have snatched it—

I pounded barefoot, clad only in my borrowed towel, into the parking lot. I looked left, right, for any signs of the demon—

—or Henry had given it back to her willingly. But he'd have only done that if . . .

Softly, in the background of our connection, I heard Henry chanting. The words weren't in English, which meant he must have been intoning some minor caltrop from the wiki-arcanum.

A momentary flash caused me to throw my arm up to shield my eyes. When the flash faded, I looked up again, to see both the driver's side and passenger side doors of Victoria's Azera open simultaneously. Henry and Victoria stepped out. Both of them stared aghast across the parking lot at me. "It's you," Victoria said. "Mikey, it's in you."

"I—that's not—"

"You lit up like a Christmas tree, doc."

I met their gazes from across the parking lot. Victoria met my gaze levelly and drew a knife from out of her top.

I sighed. I put my hands up in the air in a gesture of surrender. "I can explain," I said. "You can put that away. I'm not going to hurt you."

"Who are you?" Fister's voice joined the conversation. I turned as he skidded up into the parking lot behind me wearing only his own Rub-a-Dub's towel. He was glaring at me like I was a stranger, and even though technically I was— *technically* I wasn't his childhood friend, I just wore his body—the gaze still felt like a betrayal.

"I—I'm Dick," I said.

Part Two

Mikey

CHAPTER TWO

"Hmm," Victoria said, frowning down at my crotch. "Funny, Mikey, I'd have pegged you for a boxers kind of guy."

I stared stupidly at her for several seconds. I blinked once, twice, trying to clear the fuzz of sleep from my brain. I'd just crawled out of bed less than two minutes ago . . . what the hell was Victoria doing in my house? Why was she standing over my stove with a spatula in her hand and bacon sizzling in a frying pan on the burner?

Not that she was an unwelcome sight by any means. She was wearing a pair of my sweatpants and a white T-shirt, and by the way the morning light shone in through the half-slatted picture windows I could tell she wasn't wearing a bra. The outline of one nipple underneath the flimsy T-shirt in her profile poked me in the eye from across the room.

Seemingly oblivious to my scrutiny, she nodded at my crotch. "Please tell me you have a bathrobe.

You'll put somebody's eye out with that thing if you don't watch out."

I shook my head to clear it of the sleep fuzz. I grew aware of two things simultaneously: my state of undress . . .

. . . that, and my morning wood standing at attention inside my underwear.

At that moment Henry skidded into the room from the back hallway that led off toward my guest bedroom. He caught sight of me and immediately shielded his eyes with the back of his hand. "Whoa, Doc M! Dude . . . I mean . . . damn, dude."

I tried to shield myself by cupping my hands in front of my crotch—rather vainly, unfortunately. With the raging tent in my underwear, there was not really anywhere I could place my hands so as to hide my tumescence. I experimented with a couple of different configurations , and when I realized I was failing miserably I settled for strategically backing down the hallway that led toward my bedroom. "Wha—what are you two doing in my house?" I said. "What the—"

My undignified retreat was cut off a moment later as I backed into Fister. He'd padded up the hallway toward me, and in my state of absorption at finding Victoria and Henry both in their pajamas in my condo at six thirty in the morning, I'd failed to register his presence. But as I bumped into him, I yelped and turned around, and then when I realized in so doing I was flashing my ass-cheeks to both Henry and Victoria in the kitchen, I whirled around again.

"Mikey, a thong? Really?" Fister shook his head and chuckled. "I guess we all wanna feel pretty when we go to bed, huh?" He shuffled around me in the tight corridor, and as he passed me gave me a playful slap on my left ass-cheek. "Morning, tiger," he said. And then he shuffled into the kitchen to join Henry and Victoria.

I opened my mouth to demand an explanation, then closed it again, and opted instead to salvage what little remained of my dignity. I retreated back into my bedroom, all the way into the bathroom. There, I fumbled to put the lid down on the toilet. In my still sleep-befuddled flusterment, the lid banged down with a deafening crash. I didn't care. I sat my thong-bared ass cheeks down on the toilet and forced myself to take deep breaths.

What the fuck? What the motherfucking fuckety fuck? I wracked my memory to try to find some reason why the entire gang would be in my condo like pre-teens at a sleepover. I hadn't invited them, I was fairly certain of that. Had I?

The sleep-addlement faded far, far quicker than my morning wood. Under other circumstances, I might have spanked the problem into submission, but with Fister and Henry and Victoria—*damn*, those breasts!—only footsteps away out in my kitchen, I couldn't exactly take the matter into my hands so directly, even though the sight of Victoria's perky little nipple through her flimsy T-shirt begged for such a solution—

So not helping, I thought. Forcefully, I tried to clear my mind. I wished then that I'd taken Fister up on the Buddhist meditation classes that he'd signed up for on a lark about six months ago, because trying to get the sight of Victoria's delights out of my memory was like trying to put a jack-in-the-box back in the box after it had already sprung.

So I did the next best thing. I whipped off my underwear and climbed into my shower. I cranked it on—cold—and hopped in. I huddled in the corner and waited for my morning chubby to disappear.

And waited.

Finally, though, when my teeth were chattering from the chill of the water on my bare skin, I achieved control of my body. And since there's nothing worse than a cold shower in the morning, I quickly cranked the water to hot. I stayed in long enough for the chill to leave my body, then I got out, dried off, and peeked my head out into my bedroom.

The coast was clear here, at least. I expected my bedroom to have been invaded during the interim of my shower, but fortunately, I was able to rummage unmolested in my clothes drawers for something to wear.

Only when I was dressed in my baggiest pair of jeans did I head back out to the kitchen. By that time, Fister, Victoria, and Henry were all seated around the table in my breakfast nook enjoying a fine breakfast. They looked for all the world like a normal family sitting down to a casual breakfast—except they weren't my family . . .

I took the fourth seat around my square table. A quick round of surreptitious gazes and furtive glances made a circuit and a half around the table. Nobody seemed to want to make eye contact with me, and for my part, I couldn't quite look any of them in the eye, either.

Fortunately, Henry broke the silence first. "Here, Doc," he said, passing me a plate loaded with crispy strips of bacon and sausages. "Mom makes a mean breakfast." The hints of a sly grin spread at the corners of his mouth. "The sausage is especially . . . thick."

Victoria missed nary a beat in reaching over and slapping him on the back of the head even as he snickered at his own innuendo. At the same time, she glared at Fister across the table from her, and he obligingly aborted his own echoing snicker. With effort, he summoned a straight face, though he only managed to keep it by hunching lower over his plate of fried eggs and focusing intently on breaking the yolks with his fork.

The sausages really did look amazing, and I realized that I was famished. So I helped myself to four slices of bacon, three sausage links, then wordlessly accepted the small plate of fried eggs and fried potatoes that Victoria passed to me. Then, I reached across the table and grabbed the last two remaining slices of toast from a plate there.

I was halfway through buttering my toast before I managed to say, feigning nonchalance, as if I were merely inquiring about the weather, "Sooooo . . . you wanna tell me what the hell you're all doing in my house?"

They all three traded glances, as if silently drawing straws. Henry lost. "You mean you don't remember?" he said.

"I think I'd remember if I'd invited you over to stay the night," I said. "Not that I would do such a thing on a Wednesday." I glanced over at Henry.

"On a school day," I added pointedly. "Please don't tell me . . .there's not . . . I mean, you haven't . . . it's not . . ."

"Of course it is," Henry said. "What else would it be?"

Demons, I thought, and shivered. Things had been so quiet after we'd defeated the Holy Mother and foiled her plot to booby-trap sex for the giant mass of heterosexual men everywhere. I'd actually almost been lulled into believing that I could lead a normal life again.

Almost . . .

"I got an IM from one of Morpheus's online contacts last night about ten o'clock," Henry continued, "that indicated you might be in danger. So we all drove over here to check on you. When we got here, you were already asleep, so we just . . . let ourselves in."

"In danger?" I said. "Me? What . . . why me? I mean . . . just me? Not the rest of you?"

Henry spread his hands. "What can I say? Demons work in mysterious ways. I'm afraid that's about all I know at the moment."

"But don't worry," Victoria put in. "We'll follow up on it today. We'll get it sorted."

"You don't think . . . maybe . . . should I stay home today?" I absently took a bite of sausage. "I mean, if I'm in danger—"

"I doubt any demons will try anything in broad daylight," Fister said. "Nah, don't let on like you suspect anything. You should go to work like normal. I mean, there's all kinds of D-listers who need their buttholes examined."

I inwardly breathed a sigh of relief. I had an appointment for a follow-up consultation on Pat Robertson's anismus today, and it would be a total bitch to reschedule. Not to mention Donny Osmond's rectal prolapse . . .

"All right," I said, "but is there anything I can do? "I've got a hole in my schedule at eleven."

Fuck. I could tell by all three of their unison grins that I'd set them up perfectly without even realizing it. Normally, I'd have paid more attention than that. But they'd all caught me by surprise this morning . . .

"You're a proctologist, Mikey." By some unspoken accord, Victoria drew the privilege of delivering the zinger: "Isn't that all you've got is holes in your schedule?"

After I got over the initial shock of having the comfortable bubble of my morning routine penetrated and punctured, I was actually kind of touched by my friends' concern. After all, they'd dropped everything they were doing last night and come driving over to my house with the only thought on their minds being my safety—if you overlooked the breaking and entering, of course.

Either that, a pernicious, nagging voice in the back part of my brain cut in, *or they were just out of groceries and knew your fridge would be stocked.*

It was an uncharitable thought, though, and I banished it. I arrived at my clinic in a rather chipper mood. I greeted Elian and Dolores, my hyper-efficient front office staff, and threw myself into my day with vigor. *Bring on the bungholes*, I thought, and grinned.

"You have nothing to worry about, Mr. Robertson," I found myself reassuring Pat Robertson just slightly before eleven o'clock as I walked him personally back to the waiting room. I tried to walk all my patients back to the waiting room after their treatments or consultations—except Kirk Cameron, of course, who I usually just left alone in waiting room three to rub one out with all my implements. I'd gotten that little practice from my dad, who always used to say it was the little things like that that showed your patients they were more than just assholes to you. "In fact," I continued, "I'm confident that you'll be back to regular bowel movements again before you can say 'hallelujah.'"

His face tried to smile, I think. It looked more like a botox-impeded twitch, unfortunately. In person and up close, without the benefit of his coterie of makeup artists and stylists, he looked like refried death. In fact, I had to stifle a kamikaze giggle as I imagined him in a black robe and hunching over a scythe. He'd be a dead ringer for the grim reaper—except . . . slouchier.

"Good news, doc," he said. "Praise—"

I cut him off. "Just keep following the exercise regimen I prescribed, and I'm sure you'll feel full of shit again in no time."

"That's . . . such a relief. At my age—"

"Oh, pish." I grinned my most effervescent grin and made a gesture as if to swat his concern away.

"I'm sure you've got plenty of shit still left in you, you old devil you."

I waved him on out of the waiting room with a handful of further platitudes, then turned to find Dolores frowning over the tops of her half-framed spectacles at me. She raised an eyebrow archly. "What's gotten into you today, doc?" she asked.

"What? Too much?" I said. "You don't think he caught on, do you?"

"That senile old coot? Oh, hell, no. They don't come much more oblivious than that."

"Then what is it?" I asked. "Not funny? I've been saving up my best material all week just for him."

"No, that was a pretty good one, doc."

"Then what?"

"I don't know. You're feeling kind of . . . spunky today." She narrowed her eyes. "Did you get laid last night?"

"Oh. My. God!" Elian shuffled up, punctuating every word. Elian was a consummate professional with patients, but every once in a while, when the waiting room was empty like this, his drag queen alter ego, Ms. Perky Marilyn LeDoux, which he performed onstage Wednesday nights at the Coxbury, shone through. "Doctor M, you didn't!" He thumped me playfully on the middle of my chest with the backs of his fingertips. "I didn't know you were seeing anyone."

I feigned offense. "What makes you think I'm seeing someone?" I said. "Maybe I had a one-night stand."

Elian and Dolores both exchanged a look. Then, in unison, they both looked back at me, and Dolores spoke for the both of them: "Yeah, right."

"I could have," I said defensively. "I mean, I'm a doctor. Chicks totally dig that."

"Mmmm-hhmmm," Dolores said. She shot Elian a look, and together they returned to typing at their computers.

Elian and Dolores had both been with my practice for years, and they were great at their jobs, but sometimes . . . sometimes I just wished for office staff that didn't treat me as if I were an open book. A particularly boring open book, at that. I wondered if Bruce Wayne ever felt like this. At least he was smart enough to have a butler who knew how totally badass he really was.

Oh, well. I'd just have to content myself with knowing that I'd saved the world from the ravages of demons—twice now. Hell, it was only because Fisty, Henry, Victoria and I had taken out the Holy Mother about a month ago that people could still have one-night stands.

"Well . . . we don't have any appointments till afternoon," I said. "I'm going to go take a nap in examination room two. 'Cause . . . you know . . . it was a long night last night. Of totally wild sex."

"Whatever you say, doc," Dolores said, still typing away at her computer.

I retreated to examination room two. There, I obsessive-compulsively straightened the white paper covering on the examination table. I wasn't really tired, though, so I sat in my office chair in the corner. I crossed my legs and stared at the medical model of the rectum on the table beside me. I should be using this time to catch up on paperwork, but instead I pulled out my iPhone. I opened up the calendar app and examined my schedule. It had all my appointments, of course, not to mention my Toastmasters meeting for tomorrow evening. Everything perfectly laid out and organized.

I pulled up Friday. There, from seven o'clock in the evening, I'd scheduled MOVIE NIGHT, just as I had every Friday night for the past three months. This month's offering was *The River Wild*, because I was making my way systematically through the oeuvre of Kevin Bacon. On a whim, I erased MOVIE NIGHT and typed in instead: ONE-NIGHT STAND. Maybe it was finally time to go try speed-dating like Fister was always encouraging me to do. According to Fisty, all I had to do was say I was a doctor— which was utterly true—and it was an instant poon magnet to the over-thirty single women crowd. An M.D. was even better than a bubble butt or a six-pack or even a killer pair of dimples when it came to single women my age who were feeling the inexorable passage of time and the siren lure of security and stability.

I imagined walking into the basement of the Presbyterian Church, smiling confidently around at all the singles and knowing that I could have my pick of the litter that night. Maybe I'd find some curvaceous redhead with a perky bust and a killer smile . . .

Fuck. My imagination—the one in my head, that is—had unwittingly conjured an image of Victoria. And the imagination that resided in my pants responded in kind. And unknowingly I'd already sailed past the point of no return where trying to shut off the processional of mental images was nigh impossible.

Oh well. I knew well enough where this ship would need to put into port. I reached over and locked the door to the examination room, then pulled down my pants, freeing my . . . imagination.

And was it just my imagination, or was everything down there just a little bit . . . *more* than usual? Maybe it was just the kind of day I was having, but all the colors of my world seemed just a little bit brighter. The veins just a little bit veinier purple, the knob just a bit more swollen red . . .

My imagination conjured a vision of Victoria as Fräulein Maria in The Sound of Music running through the Alps singing "The hills are alive . . ."—because that was the best visual I could come up with when life seemed just a little bit too technocolor for reality—except instead of a nun's habit Victoria was wearing the T-shirt she'd been wearing as she stood over my stove this morning, displaying underneath a maddening little hint of . . .

Three short, sharp buzzes in quick succession brought the sound of music in my imagination to a screeching halt. *Shit! Mother of Jesus H. freaking Christ shit!* It was my office staff's signal for emergency. Usually it meant Fister. I thanked my lucky stars I'd remembered to lock the door.

But instead, a second later, Henry's voice came piping through the intercom to me. "Doctor M, Doctor M, we've got a medical emergency out here. You'd better come right away. Justin Bieber is here.

He sprained his sphincter trying to pull another fifteen minutes of fame out of his ass."

Henry? What the ever-loving fuck was he doing here? With a groan, I pulled up my pants, tucking myself gingerly into my work khakis, made sure to fasten my white lab coat around my midriff, and exited examination room two.

I found Henry in the waiting room, alone with Dolores and Elian. Dolores had a rather unrestrained look of annoyance on her face. She hated kids, which is why she'd gotten out of a pediatric office faster than a spray of explosive diarrhea. Elian looked highly bemused. "Ah, Doc," he said, "you've got a. . . em . . . friend here to visit you."

The questions I had for Henry tumbled over themselves in their haste to be uttered. "Henry? What are you doing here? How did you get here? Shouldn't you be in school?" Holmes Middle was a long way from here . . .

Henry shrugged. "I never actually went to school today. What the hell . . . it's just the standardized testing window, anyway. I took the bus here. It wasn't far. I never actually went home after waking up at your place this morning."

Both Dolores and Elian buried their heads in their computer screens, but I caught their sideways glances at this bit of information, and I replayed in my head the entire tongue-in-cheek conversation I'd just had with them not ten minutes ago about the one-night stand I'd had last night. I opened my mouth to stammer some kind of explanation. "I—I—"

"So this is your office, huh?" Henry said, casting an interested look around. "Cool. Can I see the examination rooms? Do you have those . . . those . . . hell, I don't know what they're called . . . those legs-up things like my mother has?"

"Stirrups," I said. "They're called . . . no, I don't have stirrups."

"Mmm," Henry said. "Too bad."

"Henry . . . what the hell are you doing here?"

He cocked his head in a very poorly disguised nod at Elian and Dolores, a motion that said as plain as day: *not in front of the muggles.*

"Right," I said, and took a deep breath. "Why don't you go on back into examination room two? I'll be right behind you."

Henry did as he was bid. In his wake, I turned to Elian and Dolores. "He's . . . he's . . . he's such a pain in the ass, really. He's my nephew."

Dolores arched an eyebrow at me. "You don't say, doc," she said. "You never mentioned you had a sibling."

Fuck, I thought. She had me there. I pulled my hands out of the pockets of my lab coat and spread them helplessly.

Which was even worse, because Dolores's attention went immediately to the bulge in my pants, and her eyes went round.

"I—" I stammered. Finally, I gave up trying to fish for an explanation and slinked off back to examination room two. There, I found Henry staring in fascination at the plastic medical model of the rectum. "What is it, Henry, that's so urgent?" I demanded.

"We need to go," Henry said.

"Go? Go where?"

"To rescue Fister and my mom.   They're in trouble."

CHAPTER THREE

"Okay," I said to Henry once we were safely inside my car and on the road, with no prying ears around, "on a scale of one to ten, just exactly how much trouble are Fister and your mother in?"

Henry considered. "On a scale of one to ten?" he mused. "Probably about a sixty-nine."

I shook my head. "Your gift for hyperbole never ceases to amaze me." What other answer should I have expected from a thirteen-year-old?

Henry frowned. "Hyperbole? What's that?"

"It means exaggeration."

"Who's exaggerating? It's a sixty-nine, 'cause they're probably in enough trouble that it sucks to be them no matter which way you look at it." It was my turn to frown then. I cocked my head to the side to consider his words, and I caught Henry grinning. "See what I did there?" he said.

That's a relief, I thought. If Henry was cracking jokes, it couldn't be the end of the world. At least not quite yet. Though considering what the four of us had all been through together, the end of the world probably wasn't far off. "So spill," I told him. "What do you know?'

"Not much. I got this text from Fister about an hour ago, and I headed straight over to your office." As I pulled up at a red light, he handed me his iPhone. I took it and frowned at the screen.

I frowned. "'Need fuckup?'"

"Backup, I'm assuming," Henry said. "Damn autocorrect. Either that, or he was specifically requesting you. Either way . . ."

"Ha ha," I said, and continued reading.

The message ended there. I handed the iPhone back to Henry as the light turned green again and I accelerated. "'Mikey and dick?'" I said.

"Um . . . he probably meant 'and quick.' He was typing fast before they got captured, after all. Either that, or—"

"I get it," I cut him off. "What did he mean by 'bring protection . . . coven?' You don't think that was an auto-correct for 'condom', do you?"

I grinned, slightly pleased with my own wit, but when I took my eyes off the road for only a brief moment to glance over at Henry in my passenger seat he was scowling and shaking his head as if I were a particularly obnoxious freshman pledge in a fratpack of seniors. "Why the hell would anyone bring a condom for protection against demons?" Henry said.

"Well . . . you never know," I said defensively. "I mean . . . you know. Like Fister should have been wearing a condom that time he splooged in my eye."

Henry shook his head. "He didn't splooge in your eye, if you remember, he splooged on the ceiling and it dropped in your eye. Most demonic ejaculations would blow a hole clean through the tip of a condom."

"All right, then," I said, slightly nettled at getting the pedantic treatment from someone with likely only a handful of pubes to his name. "So what do you think he meant by 'coven?'"

"That part's easy," Henry said. "We need to pay a visit to some old friends."

I put the car in park and squinted through the dual filter of sunlight and the red haze of my Spidey-sense at the run-down little shop in a backwater strip mall in Los Alamitos. WYRD SISTERS' USED BOOKS said the sign overhead. "'When shall we three meet again?'" I muttered to myself.

I hadn't really meant the comment for Henry's ears, but then, I hadn't exactly muttered it completely under my breath, either. "'Three?'" Henry said as he climbed out of the passenger seat and slammed my car door shut. "What are you talking about, 'three?' There's only two of us. I mean, it's just you and me, right? Why would there be three of us?"

I turned to frown at him. "Are you okay?" I said. It wasn't like Henry to babble. "You're acting awfully weird. Weirder than normal, I mean."

"I'm fine," Henry said. "But you're just saying some really weird shit."

"It's *Macbeth*," I said. "You know. That Scottish play?"

Henry blinked at me, uncomprehending.

"You know, the three witches from *Macbeth*. The weird sisters . . . it's Shakespeare. It's the first line from the play: 'When shall we three meet again? In lightning, thunder, or in rain?'"

"Oh," Henry said, obviously relieved. He glanced up at the clear blue sky. "How 'bout in southern California sunshine? Come on. They're waiting for us."

"Who's 'they?'" I wondered out loud, but Henry didn't bother to answer me. Instead, he led me across the tiny parking lot, up onto the token sidewalk, and across the threshold into the store. My Spidey-sense thrummed at me; there were definitely some demonic energies swirling around in this store. But the tableau that greeted me inside was nothing at all out of the ordinary. Rows and rows of wooden paperback-lined racks were arranged in a swirling mandala-like shape leading toward a counter with a ticker-tape register at the back of the shop. PAPERBACK ROMANCE 3-FOR-2 SPECIAL ALL COVERS WITH GUYS IN KILTS read a hand-inked sign on a normal sheet of letter-sized paper hanging on the end of the bookshelf nearest me. The next shelf over had a similar sign: PAPERBACK FANTASY $2.00 OFF ALL COVERS WITH HOODED ASSASSINS. And, one more bookshelf over: PARANORMAL - BADASS BITCHES WITH TRAMP STAMPS. PAY FULL PRICE AND LIKE IT.

Henry advanced into the store, and I followed behind him. As I did so, the belled door clanged as it shut behind me. I thought that this might summon a clerk who was not in immediate view, most likely hidden somewhere in the labyrinthine clusterfuck of bookshelves, but instead all it summoned was a rather disinterested-looking gray cat that stalked out from behind one of the bookshelves, glanced at Henry and me as it crossed our path, then continued on its way toward the opposite corner of the store.

"Graymalkin!" I heard a voice call. "Graymalkin, are you playing with that fucking bell again?"

And then a figure materialized to match the voice. No surprise, it was a plumpish woman, fifty-ish, her hair dyed impossibly dark black, most likely to conceal the gray in it that should have matched a trio of whiskers on her chin. She was wearing a frumpy brown T-shirt with a stegosaurus on it talking to a T-rex. It read: CURSE YOUR SUDDEN BUT INEVITABLE BETRAYAL. When she caught sight of Henry and me, she stopped, blinked once, twice at us. Then said: "Customers?" It was a question. I took it that she wasn't used to getting too many customers in this place.

Henry looked to me, then took the lead and stepped forward to address the woman. "We're here to see the coven," he announced, and met her gaze levelly. "It's about a . . . a thing."

She lowered her head to consider Henry over the tips of her horn-rimmed glasses. "Oh dear," she said. "Morpheus sent you?"

Henry nodded.

"He didn't say you'd be so young."

"I'm seventeen," Henry said. "I just look young for my age."

"Oh," the woman said. "I see." Then, she looked past Henry to me. What she saw seemed to take her aback, which was rather disconcerting to me, because I was wearing my sunglasses to mask the glowing eye of my Spidey-sense. She raised her left hand to her mouth to stifle a slight gasp. "Oh dear," she said. "It's you. I never expected to see you again."

I couldn't help it: I raised my eyebrows up over the tops of my Oakleys. "Have we met?"

"Oh, I'm sure you wouldn't remember it, dear. But that's all right." She addressed herself back to Henry. "I guess Morpheus did send you. Come."

She led us through the twisting weave of bookshelves, past John Grishams and Stephen Kings and James Pattersons and even past a small, untidy erotica section. Our trajectory through the narrow aisles between bookshelves took us past three more cats, all of which regarded us with casual disinterest. Two of the three couldn't even be bothered to get out of our way, so we had to follow our guide's lead and step over them.

She led us on a circuitous route to the back of the store. There, she stepped through a tiny door marked "SISTERS ONLY." Henry followed her through without missing a beat; I hesitated a second, however—I couldn't help it. So far, the Wyrd Sisters merely seemed . . . well, weird, but given the thrumming of my Spidey sense at the energies it was sensing in this place, I couldn't help suffering a gooseflesh-inducing premonition of *Fair is foul, and foul is fair*.

The sisters' clubhouse—for so my mind interpreted the scene I found on the other side of the threshold in the private nether parts of the bookshop—was a cozy affair, obviously for the serious coven. Judging by the ring of faintly musty-smelling, thrift store threadbare armchairs spaced equidistantly around the perimeter of the room and the additional half-dozen or so cats lounging either on laps or on the circular rug that covered the majority of the scuffed wooden floor in the middle of the circle of armchairs—thirteen of them, I registered without surprise—the sisters had been nesting here for quite some time.

Twelve of the armchairs were occupied already, and the frumpy woman who had escorted us here motioned for Henry and me to stand in the center of the circle, then silently slipped into the thirteenth armchair as our arrival drew the attention of her sisters. All around the circle, mostly middle-aged women put down their individual avocations: knitting, a romance novel featuring a bare-chested stud in a kilt, a laptop, the newest Janet Evanovich, a book of Sudoku puzzles. . . . In two instances our arrival interrupted the light nap of two of the sisters; sensing something afoot, they shook off their slumber and straightened their postures in their armchairs to see what had disturbed their rest.

The sisters' scrutiny of us was now absolute. I shifted uncomfortably. It made me feel vaguely like a wayward Padawan subjected to the shakedown of the entire council of Jedi Masters—if the Jedi Council were a pack of mostly bespectacled spinsters, that was. I opened my mouth to offer something by way of greeting, then abruptly closed it again.

As I'd expected, one of their number, the oldest of the lot at about mid-fifties, I judged, served as the spokeswoman—or *spokeswitch*, my mind interjected. "Well," she said, looking over the tops of her bifocals at me, "I never expected to see you again."

I frowned. This was getting unnerving. "You have me at a disadvantage," I said. "I'm afraid I don't recall—"

"No, of course you wouldn't," she said, "which believe me, is all for the best. And who might this be?" She focused on Henry. "Not your son, surely?"

"No," I said. "He's . . .ahm . . . he's my . . ."

"His nephew," Henry cut in. "He's my uncle. My uncle Mikey."

"I see," the woman said, in a tone that suggested she'd already lost interest. "But what of your partner?" she asked.

I blinked. "My partner?"

"The one who brought you here last time. Your boyfriend . . .?"

"Boyfriend?"

"Yeah. You know. Nice abs. Works out. Cute dimples. Hung like a—"

"You mean Fister?" I said. How the hell could Fister have brought me here without my remembering it?

She pursed her lips. "Well, that's a bit of an overshare, sweetie, but I guess so."

Henry took a step forward. "It's about him that we've come," he said. "He's in trouble, and we need to help him."

The woman sighed. "Couldn't leave well enough alone, that one, could he? Still, can't say as I'm all that surprised. Demons, I take it?"

Henry nodded.

"Noble of you to want to intervene on your friend's behalf, but foolish, I'm afraid. If he can't keep his cute little ass away from demons, I'm afraid he'll get himself killed sooner or later."

"We'd prefer later, if you don't mind," Henry said. "Will you help us?"

The matron leaned forward in her chair. "And just what is it you would ask of us, little man?" she said.

Henry met her gaze levelly. "The *Macarena Incantatem*."

All thirteen of the sisters sucked in their breaths in unison. The spokeswitch leaned back in her chair and studied Henry thoughtfully, then said, "Are you certain you know what it is you ask, my boy?"

Henry nodded. "We wouldn't ask if it wasn't important."

The assembled sisters traded a flurry of nervous looks. I took advantage of their preoccupation to whisper sideways to Henry, "What's the *Macarena Incantatem*?"

"It's a spell," Henry whispered.

"No shit. I gathered that much. What kind of a spell?"

"A pretty badass one."

Which wasn't particularly helpful, I thought, annoyed. But I supposed Henry knew what he was doing. As his online persona, Morpheus, Henry had written at least half of the wiki-bestiary. "The *Macarena Incantatem*" sounded like his trademark bastardized Latin seasoned with a sprinkle of Harry Potter lingo.

Unfortunately, my round of twenty questions with Henry was over. The sisters had quelled their fleeting incredulity and had returned to staring at us. "That's quite a powerful spell, young man," the spokeswitch said.

"But you can do it?" Henry said. It wasn't entirely a question; he spoke these words with a hint of a challenge. "You're the most powerful coven in the greater Los Angeles area. I would hate to have to go to the Sisters of Perpetual Sorrow."

The spokeswitch hissed in unison with at least half of her sisters. "Those uppity schoolgirl bitches? They can't handle a spell of that magnitude."

"Maybe. Maybe not. Between you and me, they're a bit too emo for my tastes. Still, they're totally hot." Henry shrugged. "We could always go ring them . . ."

It was surely an empty threat. I knew it, Henry knew it, and even the Wyrd Sisters must have known it. But I had to hand it to Henry, he sure knew how to play on vanity. The throng of sisters held a committee meeting comprised entirely of wordless glances around the circle. Finally, the spokeswitch said, "Very well. We shall perform the incantation on your friend, and only on him." She nodded to me.

"Wait, what?" Henry said. "No way. You can't. It has to be on both of us."

She shook her head. "You are far too young."

Henry took a step nearer to her. "Look, I know I'm young. But you can't—I can't go into this nest of demons without the protection of the *Macarena Incantatem*. It'd be suicide."

"Then you shall have to resort to plan B." The spokeswitch considered me again, and the expression of benevolent disdain on her face made it apparent that she'd found me lacking. "Or hope that you've chosen your associates wisely. Morpheus."

Henry, for the first time, took a half a step backward. He looked a little flustered. "What? Morpheus? Me?" he managed to feign some incredulity, but it was too little, too late. He visibly searched for further words, but eventually settled for a halfhearted, "Ah, fuck."

"You should've let me do the talking," I muttered sideways to Henry.

"Fear not," the spokeswitch said. "We shall not betray your secret. We're on the same side, my boy. Knowing your true identity changes nothing . . . well, almost nothing. I suppose Sister Helen," she shot a look across the circle at a dowdy member of her coven, "may have to alter her Morpheus online fanfiction a little."

Henry looked to the indicated sister. "Sister Helen? You're cunnybunny1368?" He sketched her a gallant little mock-bow. "That shit's totally hot." She flushed like a schoolgirl at the praise.

Then Henry turned back to the spokeswitch. "Look, if you know I'm Morpheus, then you must know I haven't just been hiding behind a computer screen all the time. I may be young, but I've seen real demons. I—we—" He gestured to include me, "we've taken out our share of some pretty nasty mofos. Just last month we took down the Holy Mother."

The spokeswitch held up a hand to forestall further rhetoric from Henry. "Nobody's doubting your prowess, Morpheus. Though your language leaves a lot to be desired. Indeed, you have our respect, especially with all you've accomplished for someone so young—"

"Then you've gotta pee on me!" Henry said.

I did a double take. "Wait, what?" I said. "Pee on you?"

"On us, I mean," Henry corrected. At my blank look, he added, "Geez, doc, what did you think the *Macarena Incantatem* was?" He turned back to address the spokeswitch. "I know it's a little kinky, and I'm kind of underage and shit, but believe me . . . it's necessary."

"This has nothing to do with you being underage," the spokeswitch said. "Magic on the level of the *Macarena Incantatem* . . . it's too powerful. It changes you." She pointed to me. "He's old enough to know who he is. He has a fighting chance of keeping his identity intact. You, my boy, I'm afraid—"

"Wait a minute," I said. I stepped in front of Henry and addressed myself to the spokeswitch to forestall an epic teenager-grandmotherish blowout. "What is this? This spell changes the recipient? How?"

"There is no physical harm—"

"That's not what I'm worried about. Tell me what you mean by 'changes.'"

The spokeswitch spread her hands. "We can't be certain. We've never attempted the *Macarena Incantatem* before. But according to the Arcanum, it may overwhelm the identity of the recipient. It may cause . . . changes."

"That's it? That's all you know? You're basing your refusal on some pretty scant information."

"We respect the Arcanum—"

"But all that aside," I continued, steamrolling her, "surely you've realized good ol' Morpheus here can be a pushy, foul-mouthed little prick. Half the time he's insufferable and the other half he needs a good old-fashioned ass-whupping. Now all I can say is if this spell just might happen to cause personality shifts, then I'll take my chances. It might just be an improvement. So will you just pee on the kid, for Christ's sake? Our friends may be running out of time."

There was a moment of silence as the sisters considered my appeal with another silent conclave of looks and glances among themselves. While they conferred, I turned to look at Henry. His eyes were wide, and his eyebrows arched high. "Gee, doc . . . thanks?" His tone was somewhat questioning, but I decided to take his gratitude at face value.

"You owe me one, kid," I said.

The Wyrd Sisters had apparently finished their silent conferral. "Very well," the spokeswitch said, "but be it on your head."

"Actually," Henry cut in, "be it on his face, if you wouldn't mind."

I traded an exasperated look with the spokeswitch. "See what I mean?"

The spokeswitch rose from her armchair and addressed herself to her sisters. "Come on, ladies. We have a spell to prepare." Then, she turned back to Henry and me. She licked her lips. "Take off your clothes," she ordered us.

Henry and I did as she ordered. Both of us were bashful at first, cupping our hands in front of our privates, but it appeared we needn't have bothered. After the members of the coven rolled up the rug covering the middle of the floor in the circle and laid down a plastic tarp (ready for anything, apparently—they'd claimed not to have ever cast this spell before, but they must have dabbled in all kinds of black magic which could have a tendency to get a bit messy), the sisters began doing likewise. "You might want to close your eyes," I whispered to Henry. "This could get a little . . . saggy."

"You're not kidding," Henry muttered. "Once. . . just once I'd like to see a naked woman that doesn't give me nightmares."

I couldn't blame him. As a medical practitioner, I was more accustomed to the sight of the human body in all its many-splendored glory. Fortunately, there was nothing on display here than was any more cringeworthy than Pat Robertson's bony octogenarian ass bent over in front of me waiting for me to probe it, as I had just this morning—though there were some close seconds.

"Lie down," the spokeswitch instructed us, "and get comfortable. We'll have to prime the energies first. It might take a while."

Prime the energies? I wondered if that was sorceress-speak for something. Unfortunately, they were all about their business and not apparently in the mood to answer questions. As Henry and I did as we were bid, one of the sisters dimmed the lights while a half-dozen or so lit candles around the periphery of the circle where Henry and I lay. Once I got used to the feel of the plastic tarp on my bare backside, it was easy enough to relax, so I rested my hands lightly over my privates for that one tiny little bit of modesty, and looked up at the ceiling.

When all the candles were lit, the sisterhood all joined hands and formed a circle around Henry and me. Then, they started chanting. I'd expected the power phrases from the *Macarena Incantatem* to be in Latin, which I had a passing familiarity with due to all the vocabulary I'd had to learn in med school, but I recognized none of the words or roots that I heard, so I spent a handful of minutes of my leisure trying to identify the language of their chanting. I ultimately failed.

"Ever been golden showered before, doc?" Henry asked me as the Wyrd sisters' chanting intensified in volume.

"Afraid not," I said.

"Well, hey, first time for everything, right?"

"I guess. I mean, how bad can it be?" I paused. "What's this spell for, anyway?"

"Well, theoretically, the *Macarena Incantatem* is supposed to mask the scent of the recipients from demons, making them practically undetectable to demon nostrils. And it's also supposed to provide protection from demons' . . . you know."

I frowned. "No, I don't know. Protection from demons' what?"

"Their . . . you know. Fluids. And stuff. The *Macarena Incantatem* in the Middle Ages was a fairly common countermeasure used after demon rapes to prevent the conception of demon babies."

I grimaced. "Are we likely to get raped by demons where we're going?"

"How the hell should I know? But better to be safe than sorry, right? It's kind of like Achilles . . . you know, in that Brad Pitt movie."

I hadn't actually seen the Brad Pitt movie he was referring to, but I was familiar with the legend of Achilles from mythology. "I see," I said. "So make sure they cover the heel."

"Well, yeah, except the heel is pretty easy to get in this case," Henry said. "I mean, it's not like they have to dip us in a vat or anything."

"Well, that's a relief," I muttered.

"But we'd probably better be on the safe side and make sure to open our mouths when they spray on our faces. You know. Coat the throat."

Just in case we get throat-raped by a demon, I thought, and shuddered. Even at his young age,

Henry had been doing this whole demon fighting thing much longer than I had; he was eminently practical, and highly detail-oriented.

"Shhhh!" one of the Wyrd sisters who stood over us hissed during a lull in the chanting. Duly chastised, I bit back my reply to Henry, and held my silence.

I didn't have to wait long. The coven brought their chanting to a cacophonous crescendo. My inner eye thrummed with the awareness of power crackling in the air of the room; it was like an invisible torrent swimming in the air just waiting to be unleashed.

And then the waterworks started. One of the sisters straddled me, and at that moment I was quite thankful for the dim lighting in the room. Nevertheless, I closed my eyes and braced for impact. Her blessing came forward in a strong stream that gushed first onto my chest. It was warm, as I'd expected—no, it was *hot*, burning, in fact, far hotter than human urine should have been. Whatever otherworldly power the sisters had called forth to imbue their urine felt like bathing in acid. I opened my mouth to cry out, but in that instant another of the sisters straddled my face and let fly, and I needn't have reminded myself to open my mouth as Henry had suggested. It flowed into my throat, and I coughed and gagged and hacked—

—and then finally it was over. The shadows disappeared from above me. A moment later a third sister appeared and began discharging herself, but she aimed at my navel and worked down, and as my splutterings of surprise tapered away, I realized my body had adapted, much as your skin grows used to the scalding heat of a bubbling hot tub, not when you first step in, but after you've sunk down in it for a while, until it's so comfortable on your bare skin that you can't imagine stepping out again. Despite the smell, which was that of normal human urine mixed with something else of a more supernatural tinge—incense, maybe?—it was really quite tolerable. Pleasant, even, if you surrendered yourself to it—

—and I did. Surrender myself to it, that is. As the third sister's pittering reached my pubes, then her last dribbles spattered onto my penis, I sprang a ramrod boner the likes of which I hadn't registered since I was probably about Henry's age. My first instinct was to move my hands to cover it up out of modesty, but then I realized that that would be my own Achilles heel, so I kept my hands where they were.

The fourth sister drew up and anointed my thighs all the way down to my feet, and all the while my arousal grew in intensity. Could I reach out to stroke myself, I wondered—or would that interfere with the workings of the spell? I had no way of knowing.

"Turn over," the fifth sister instructed me as she came to continue the spell and bathe my backside in the glorious protection of the *Macarena Incantatem*. I did as she instructed, though considering my tumescence I was forced to arch my back, and couldn't lay down completely on my stomach.

Fortunately, it didn't seem to matter. The remaining sisters could straddle me just as well this way, and as the stream of the fifth pittered onto the back of my neck, I moaned in ecstasy. My body was on fire, and had become one with the heat and the sheer power contained in the sisterhood's urine . . .

. . . the sixth came and bathed my lower back down to my buttocks, and as her blessing sogged into my buttcrack I gasped with the joy of that minuscule little penetration. I longed to have it travel further inside me, all the way through my insides, suffusing my innards with its power.

And finally, the seventh, the last of the sisters apportioned to me. She finished me off, bathing from the back of my thighs down to my feet, and as the last few drops of her blessing pattered onto my toes, I could contain myself no longer: I spasmed out a blessing of my own that was—alas—destined for no greater greatness than that of the tarp beneath me.

And then it was over. I lay gasping on all fours in the aftermath, trying to catch my breath. My eyes were closed, I realized; when I could open them again I looked to my left, and made eye contact with Henry. His hair was sopping and his face was streaked with droplets of moisture, but as he made eye contact with me his face crinkled in concern. "You all right, doc?" he asked. "You sounded . . ."

I took a few deep breaths before I could answer. "You . . . you didn't feel that? It was . . . it was amazing."

Henry frowned. "It was . . . wet."

At that moment one of the sisters turned the electric lights in the chamber back on, and the sudden luminescence caused me to squint in momentary pain. I flopped over onto my back next to my own little puddle that I'd made and blinked a few times. And when my vision cohered, I realized I was staring up at the spokeswitch.

She regarded me, then looked to the puddle beside me. "Who'd have guessed?" she muttered. "You are one kinky-assed motherfucker, you know that?"

CHAPTER FOUR

"All right," I said once Henry and I were back in my car proceeding at a speed limit-appropriate velocity toward Fullerton to resume our rescue of Fister and Victoria, "What is it you're not telling me?"

Henry heaved a huge sigh, as if in regret that the game was finally up. "All right," he said, "but I hope you understand, it was for your own good."

I'll be the judge of that, I thought. "So what is it?"

"Well," Henry said, "I didn't want to tell you, but you caught me. You see, the truth is, doc . . ." He paused.

"What is it?" I nearly screeched.

"Well . . . you smell kind of funny."

"Look who's talking." The Wyrd Sisters had been kind enough to douse us down with pails of frigid water to wash the sheen of the golden shower off our skin—the protective power was in the magic of the ritual, the spokeswitch had proclaimed, and not in the urine itself; the urine was merely the medium of delivery. If that were so, I wondered why they couldn't have used a less . . . icky . . . substance, but then, what the hell did I know about arcane magic? Still, the bath at the end of the *Macarena Incantatem* had been merely perfunctory at best; there was already a miasma of long-unwashed urinals permeating the inside of my car that would take gallons of Febreeze and dozens of air fresheners to fully eradicate.

I tried to fix Henry with my best *don't bullshit me* glare, which was difficult because I couldn't really take my eyes off the road for more than an instant. "You know that's not what I meant," I said.

"All right, all right. But you gotta realize it's not my fault. My mother and Fister swore me to secrecy."

"Come on," I said. "Out with it. I deserve to know."

Henry sighed again. "All right. But promise not to tell them I told you?"

"Just spill."

"Okay, okay. My mom totally thinks you're hot."

"She does? She told you that—?" I opened my mouth to ask a half dozen questions in quick succession, then closed it again. Damn, this kid was good. "Not that," I said firmly. "Come on. You know something about why those sisters knew me, but I have no memory of ever meeting them. Tell me."

"All right," Henry said. "You remember that trip you took to Cancun with Fister about two years ago?"

"Yeah?"   To be honest, I had only fuzzy recollections of that ill-fated trip. I'd spent most of it sleeping off a bitch of a hangover from the local tequila. "What about it?" I prompted.

"Well . . . it wasn't a worm in the tequila."

I frowned. "What was it, then?"

"You don't really wanna know, trust me. Let's just say it was demonic in nature."

No more than fifteen minutes ago I'd been golden showered by a coven of saggy middle-aged women, yet *now* my stomach decided to do churny flip-flops. "So you mean I accidentally ate a demon?"

"Yeah. Believe me, it's probably a relief you can't remember much of the experience. But that's how I met Fister . . . online, of course. He tracked me down. Went to great lengths to exorcise the demon from you. And apparently, he had a h-h-heck of a time trying to find komodo dragon livers in Mexico. Even with ebay, those are a b-b-b-bit hard to come across."

I raised an eyebrow. "Are you stuttering?"

In the periphery of my rear-view mirror I caught Henry's look of concern. "I think so," he said. "Must be the *Macarena Incantatem*. Sh-sh-sh-shoot!"

"'Shoot?'" I said. "That's all you can say? 'Shoot?'"

"I—I—" Henry scrunched up his face, and seemed to be physically struggling with his own mouth. "Fuzzballs!"

"'Fuzzballs?' Now I know something's wrong. Try repeating after me: 'Fuckmonkey.'"

"F-f-f-f-flibberty gibbet!"

"Hmm. Try this one: 'cockgobbler.'"

"C-c-c-criminy!"

"All right, one more. How about 'assmunch whorespawn dicksmack-a-daisy?'"

He frowned and looked over at me. "What the h-h-heck does that mean?"

"First thing that came to me. Just try it."

"Whatever." He concentrated. "A-a-a— . . . ah, heck, doc. I can't."

"It must be the *Macarena Incantatem*," I said in my best diagnostician's tone. Though to be honest, I had my doubts. This could indeed be a side effect of the *Macarena Incantatem* . . . or given the way the spokeswitch had disapproved of Henry's foul mouth, it could just be one of their own extra little flourishes. Either way—

"You don't think it's permanent, is it? I can't go to school talking like this. I'll get my a-a-a . . . bottom kicked."

"Hmm. The sisters did say the incantation would change you. Potentially wreak havoc with your identity. Do you feel any different?"

"I feel like I need a shower. But other than that, no."

"Well, that's a relief," I said. "Considering everything, you got off pretty lucky. Other than your rather extensive lexicon of vulgarity, there doesn't seem to be any impairment with the rest of your speech. Hell, I actually think it's kind of an improvement."

Henry glared sideways at me, but let my jibe drop. "What about you, doc? Do you feel different in any way?"

I considered. "Not really. I'm older, though. My identity's firmer. More set."

"Are you horny?"

"What? What the hell does that have to do with anything?"

"Just answer the question. Are you horny?"

I shook my head. "No."

"Even if I say boo-boo-boo—*darnit!*—breasts?"

There was a sudden, uncomfortable stirring in my pants. "Stop it," I said.

"What about nice, round, fat bottoms?"

The stirring intensified into a straining inside my pants. "That's not funny," I said.

"Whatever you do, don't think about supermodels in bikinis."

"All right, stop it! So I'm horny. What does that prove? I'm a man. Men are horny. That doesn't mean anything's different."

"No. That's a relief. I was just testing to make sure your Dick was all right. I mean, you sure seemed to get off on the *Macarena Incantatem*. I was afraid—"

"Wait a minute. You said 'dick.'"

"Did I?"

"You couldn't say 'cockgobbler,' but you can say 'dick?' How the hell does that work?"

"I—I don't know."

"Say it again."

"Say what again?"

"Dick. Come on. Say it. Dick!"

"I don't think—"

"Just try it. *Dick!*"

We were stopped at a stop light. I got a nasty glare from the young couple in the Miata waiting in the turn lane next to me, but I ignored them and thumbed the button to raise my window.

"D-d-d-d—" Henry shook his head. "I can't, doc."

"But you said it once. I heard it."

"Well, that's a good sign," Henry said. "Maybe it's wearing off already." But he didn't sound convinced, and I wasn't really, either.

It was still early afternoon when we came to the address Henry had inputted into my GPS. It was an ordinary-looking factory complex in the industrial park; there was nothing on the marquee outside the front office structure, a simple trio of prefab modulars plunked end to end, altogether about the length of a football field, to suggest the actual product that was manufactured by Wizzard Industries, LLC, but judging by the crisp newness of the office prefabs I guessed they must have recently expanded. Behind the offices was the factory proper, an aging but well-kept permanent structure that I guesstimated contained at least four stories.

"What do you think?" I said to Henry. Unfortunately, given the lay of the industrial park, there were far too many lines of sight leading across the parking lot to the building. "Should we try and see if there's a back door?"

Henry considered. "Nah. I'd imagine just about everybody who comes to this place goes in the back door. We didn't drive all the way out of our way to get *Macarena Incantatemed* for nothing. Might as well just go in the main entrance. We're undetectable to demons, remember?"

"Yeah, but it's not like we're invisible," I said. "There may still be people with eyes."

Henry shrugged, apparently unconcerned. "We could take time to come up with a plan, but every moment more we waste is one more moment that they could fuh-fuh-fuh . . . do nasty things to Fister and my mother."

He had a point. My gut churned with unease at the thought of what our unknown adversaries might have already done to Fister and Victoria. They'd both gone scouting earlier this morning on my behalf . . . if anything happened to them on my account, I wasn't sure I could ever forgive myself.

Against my better judgment, I parked in the front parking lot. Henry and I got out of the car and sauntered casually up to the entrance of the middle modular. We pushed through the front door and entered.

Inside, a desk island reception area, in many ways similar to the area where Elian and Dolores worked in my own office, was curiously unmanned. I glanced at the counter and saw a sign that read: OUT TO LUNCH. Curious. I glanced at my watch. 3:37 in the afternoon . . . an odd time for a lunch.

Henry frowned. "Do you hear that?"

I perked my ears, and heard the telltale sounds of unrestrained grunting coming from an office with drawn Venetian blinds located behind the reception island. I concentrated to attempt to parse the sounds I was hearing: I could distinguish two rather distinct participants in the cacophony, one a bass, guttural *rnnnggghh rnggghhhh rnggghh*, and the other a rather high-pitched, vowel-heavy squealish *aiiiiieeee aiiiiiieeee aiiiiiieeeee*! But tonally, even the latter sounded as if it belonged to a man.

"Geez," Henry muttered. "Sounds like a stuck pig."

Henry's eyes widened, surely mirroring my own, as the telltale sounds of spanking echoed out from behind the office door. "I think that *is* a stuck pig," I muttered back. As the volume of grunting intensified, crescendoing toward the unmistakable sounds of climax, I said, "Come on. Let's not look a gift horse in the mouth." I motioned for Henry to follow me and tiptoed toward a corridor that I guessed would connect the office prefabs to the factory complex itself.

We navigated the empty tunnel about fifty feet toward a door at the end. As a precaution, Henry and I took up positions on both sides of the door and pressed our ears to it. Nothing. All was quiet on the other side. Too quiet. Henry and I traded a glance, and a pair of unison shrugs that said as clearly as words: *well, we've come this far*.

With a fervent prayer to any deity who would still acknowledge my existence that I wasn't opening the door to my death, I turned the doorknob and went inside the factory proper.

Only dim safety lighting illuminated the production floor. That, and the glowing redness of my Spidey-eye, which flared like a beacon, so sudden and so intense that it momentarily overwhelmed my more mundane sight.

"Criminy, put that out, would you?"

I kept my eyes firmly squinted closed and fished in my shirt pocket for the pair of sunglasses that I always kept handy just for instances like these. Now I knew how Cyclops from the X-Men must have felt . . .

With the sunglasses on, I squinted to try to coax back my normal vision. The shades rendered the dim interior of the factory proper even dimmer, but I could make out a random-looking warren of machinery and conveyor belts and vats that studded the production floor, giving no clue to my untrained eye what the hell this factory could possibly produce. Whatever it was, there was no shift in progress at the moment; the entire factory seemed deserted, which was decidedly odd at this time of the afternoon on a Wednesday. "Come into my parlor," I muttered, and shuddered.

"Come on," Henry said, and before I could protest, he headed into the labyrinth of machinery.

Once inside the clutter of industrial paraphernalia, my unease mounted. There were just too many nooks and crannies and crevices for creepy-crawly nasty things to hide in here. And shadows. So, so many shadows. Which creeped me the hell out even more, because—

"Do you feel like we're being watched?" I whispered as I dogged Henry's footfalls.

"Shh." Henry stopped next to what looked to be an industrial-sized laundry wringer. He held up his hand, his index finger extended to signal *wait*. And in the pulsating silence that ensued I could hear the frantic *thump thump thump* of my own heartbeat. And then Henry said, "Hide."

He didn't have to tell me twice. He and I both scuttled behind the wringer-presser thingy. We waited.

And after only a few moments I heard what he had heard: sniffing—like bloodhounds on a scent. *Christ*, I thought, *they have guard dogs. Shit shit shit* . . . I hated dogs. Ever since Mrs. McKeon's schnauzer had chased me on my way home from school in the third grade and had made me shart my pants in terror. On that fateful day, the possibility of ever becoming a postman had been irrevocably ripped from my future.

Henry and I peeked our heads out from behind the industrial presser. My first thought—that the factory was protected by guard dogs—had been somewhat right, and yet so so wrong at the same time. A pair of what could have been ordinary pygmies lumbered into view between the rows of machinery. . . they were short, maybe about four feet tall, and bipedal, but there the resemblance to men stopped. They may have walked on two legs, but the creatures had the claws and heads of dogs. Dobermans, was my guess.

I stifled a gasp. These were demons. Fully incarnated demons from the nether hells.

And they had our scent. I watched as they paused and sniffed the air. Then, they both cocked their heads to the side, as if puzzled. They perked their floppy ears, and I instinctively halted my breathing. *Time to find out if the* Macarena Incantem *is worth what we paid for it*, I thought.

At first my verdict would have leaned toward *no*, since the guard dogs—and that was apparently exactly what they were, for I saw now that they were dressed in the matching khaki uniforms of security guards, like mall cops—seemed to linger far too long in their spot only a few footsteps away from where Henry and I crouched. Sniffing the air . . . *Oh Christ, they have our scent . . .*

But then, the one on the left barked once to the other, who answered in kind. They moved on further into the labyrinth of machinery. From my hiding spot, I stared after their retreating forms. It was decidedly eerie watching two bipedal Dobermans saunter away; it would have helped my cognitive fuckadoo if they'd lumbered away on all fours or sniffed each other's butts or something, but seeing them walk upright on two legs was just . . .

"Creepy," Henry whispered, finishing my thought for me. He shuddered.

We emerged from behind the industrial presser. "Looks like the coven was worth their salt," I said. "Remind me to send them a thank-you card."

"For the spell, or the orgasm?" Henry said, and grinned. I rolled my eyes, but didn't bother to dignify his crack with a response.

"Which way?" I said, surveying the interior of the factory. I didn't really want to follow in the path of the guard dogs, but they had gone off in the direction Henry and I had been heading before they'd wandered past us.

Henry considered. "What's your Spidey sense telling you? We should head toward the greatest concentration of demonic activity."

What a fantastic idea, I thought, *head straight toward all the things that can kill you.* I shook my head. I said: "I'm a doctor, Jim, not a homing device."

Henry blinked at me. "Who the heck is Jim?"

I sighed. "We're going to have to get you a serious education in the classics, kiddo," I said.

"Whatever. But which way?"

I concentrated. My extra sense was sending out a general all-points; this whole fucking factory was riddled with demonic activity. "I don't think it matters. We just need to find out where they'd be most likely to be holding Fister and your mother." I chose a direction that would take us further into the heart of the factory, but was tangential to the trajectory of the guard dogs.

We safely navigated the production floor until we reached a wall on our right-hand side. It made me feel better: one less direction any nasty demonic thingies could come at us from. A trio of identical offices with doors next to windows with drawn venetian blinds on the other sides—what I guessed to be the floor supervisors' offices—lined the wall, spaced equidistantly. Henry stopped before the first one. "Hear that?" he said.

I cocked my ears to listen. I did indeed hear something: more grunting, similar to that which we'd heard coming from the front reception office. Henry turned sideways to press his ear to the door, and I followed suit.

The door was rather flimsy, and not particularly well soundproofed, so the noises of strenuous activity from inside were easy enough to overhear. In addition to the grunting, I could hear the sounds of flesh slapping against flesh, familiar from virtually every anal porn scene I'd ever watched.   And then, a male voice from behind the door: "You like that, you little bitch? You like that, huh?"

And in answer, another male voice: "Ay, *papi,* yes! Harder!"

I shook my head. I glanced at Henry, and wished I could have covered his ears. An odd thought, I know, considering I'd already gotten him golden showered this afternoon, but he was only thirteen . . .

Henry motioned with a tilt of his head for us to move on. I followed him to the next office door, and we paused there to put our ears to this door. Not surprisingly, more of what could have come from the same porn soundtrack, only with a less Puerto Rican accent: *You like my big cock in your ass? Oh, yes, oh yes, oh, Christ, yes*!

Henry made to move on, but I hesitated. Suddenly, a wave of déjà vu bitch-slapped me . . . or spanked my ass hard, if you will, like the *papi* behind door number one. Henry glanced at me, concerned. "What is it, doc?" he whispered.

I took a few steps away from the door so my voice wouldn't inadvertently carry to the otherwise engaged gentlemen inside the office. I frowned as I tried to pin down the source of the odd sense of been-here-done-this, but I ultimately failed. I shook my head. "I'm not sure," I told him. "But this feels really familiar somehow."

Henry held up both hands defensively. "Hey, no judgment, doc. If you go cruising gay bathhouses late at night, it's none of my business."

I raised an eyebrow. "Who said anything about gay bathhouses?"

"Not me. I mean . . . I'm just saying. Come on. We may not have much time." And he moved on to door number three.

I stared after him for a moment. Then, I shook my head and followed him.

Door number three offered a similar soundtrack. Three out of three. Damn. Whoever the hell these guys were in this factory, they were sure horny. And who could blame them? Even the mere sounds of their unbridled concupiscence caused stirrings all my own inside my pants. As Henry moved on away from door number three, I followed behind a moment later, and surreptitiously adjusted my junk so it wouldn't strain so much inside my pants—

—but not surreptitiously enough, apparently. Henry caught sight of my maneuver and raised an eyebrow. "What's the matter, doc?" he said.

"Nothing," I said. "I'm just . . . sometimes you gotta . . . you know . . . adjust."

He grinned. "I've seen the tight underwear you wear, remember? Ain't nobody could fall out of place in that. It's not that, is it? You're horny, aren't you?"

"I—" I stared at him, and then a thought blindsided me. "Oh, Christ," I muttered. "You don't think the *Macarena Incantatem* made me gay, do you?"

"You mean gayer than your comic book collection? Or a job where you finger buttholes all day? I wouldn't worry about it, doc."

"Very funny."

"Look," Henry said, "look on the bright side, will you? If the *Macarena Incantatem* made you gay, then so what? Maybe you'll get laid as a gay man more often than you do as a straight one."

I opened my mouth to protest, but then closed it again. He kind of had a point there.

"Now come on, will you?" Henry moved off again, keeping the wall on our right side.

After a few minutes of creeping in the dark we left the production floor and came to what was apparently the warehouse area of the plant. Rows and rows of identical boxes bearing the Wizzard Industries logo were neatly stacked about chest-high. "Wait a minute," I called to Henry.

He turned to me. "What is it?"

I turned to the nearest box and peeled back the packing tape sealing it. "I want to see what they're packing in this place."

Henry frowned. "Besides fudge, you mean?"

I ignored him. After a few more moments I had the box open. I reached inside and pulled out . . .

"Hmm," I muttered. "That's odd."

"What is it?" Henry asked.

I considered the puck-like object in my hands. I brought it to my nose to sniff it, and my suspicion was confirmed. "See for yourself," I said. I tossed it to Henry. "Urinal cakes."

Henry regarded the seemingly endless stacks of boxes. "That many urinal cakes? Geez, there must be, like, millions or something."

Despite Henry's normal gift of hyperbole, I had to agree with his unofficial math. Whether or not there were literally *millions* of urinal cakes packed inside the boxes, there was certainly a confirmed *fuckload*. All packed and ready to ship.

"Shoot, hide!" Henry said suddenly, and I left off my examination of the stacks of urinal cakes and did as he bid. We both scampered behind the nearest row of boxes just in time. Barely a second and a half later two more of the canine hybrid beasties came into sight. They were evidently in a hurry, because these didn't even pause to consider our scents on the air. Instead, they merely lumbered on past us, panting slightly.

Far too soon for me to consider safe, Henry left our hiding spot. "Come on." He beckoned to me. "We have to follow them."

"Are you crazy?" I whispered. "Those things . . ."

"They were on their way somewhere," Henry said to me. "I'd bet good money it's to where they're keeping Fister and my mom."

I shrugged. He could have had a point. Or, on the other hand, they could have been on their way post haste to a fancy dinner party of Kibbles and Bits. There was no way of knowing without following them.

So we did. Unfortunately, that proved easier said than done. They were keeping a stiff pace, one that Henry and I had a tough go of matching in unfamiliar territory as we were. The emergency lighting was far from ideal for these kinds of hot pursuits, and twice we nearly crashed into piles of boxes in our haste. Each near miss brought me to the verge of hyperventilating; all it would take was one misstep to bring stacks and stacks of boxes crashing down to the concrete floor . . . and that would mean the end of our tactical advantage of the *Macarena Incantatem*. I imagined the fits of vanilla-mouthed apoplexy Henry would suffer if he realized he'd given up his ability to swear for nothing.

Fortunately, though, we managed to keep the lumbering shadows of the demons in our sights just barely long enough to realize that they'd gone down a flight of stairs where the warehouse dead-ended in a wall. Henry and I drew up short at the head of the stairs and peered down.

It was infernally dark down there. Even the emergency lighting didn't penetrate down there: we'd be navigating blind. *It's a trap*! my brain shouted at me.

Henry's gung-ho decision to follow the canine-headed guards floundered, too. He hesitated, and looked to me. "Well . . ." he said, visibly marshalling his courage.

"We've come this far," I pointed out.

"Yeah," Henry said. "Once more under the bleachers."

I stared at him. "What?"

"It's something my English teacher says. Shakespeare, or something."

"Oh. You mean 'once more unto the breach, dear friends?'"

"Something like that." He took a deep breath. "Come on."

I followed him down the stairwell. Even the faintly reassuring sliver of emergency lighting faded as we descended, plunging us into total darkness, and we had to feel out each step with our toes lest we tumble down them, and then, when we reached the bottom, continue with our hands in front of us like insect feelers—

"Hey!" Henry cried, "quit grabbing my b-b-bottom!"

"'Bottom?'" I said. "Don't tell me you can't even say 'butt?' Geez, those witches really did a number on you."

"I'll say, doc."

"That must mean the spell was context-specific. Surely you've gotta be able to use 'but' as a conjunction. Try it."

"If I do, will you be quiet?"

"Sorry. I guess I babble when I'm nervous."

"Yeah, no kidding. How about this: 'I prefer not to chew my food, *but munch.*' Hey, that actually worked."

"'Buttmunch?'" I said. "You're totally cheating."

"Will you shut your *as*-phalt, you *count*-ry bumpkin?"

"Now you're just being obnoxious."

There appeared to be room for us both to walk abreast here, so I drew even with Henry. At least I thought so. "Henry!" I whispered. "Where are you?"

"Right next to you," he responded. "Here. Can you feel my hand?"

I stabbed around in the darkness, and at last managed to grab hold of his hand.

"I think I preferred you when you were molesting me," Henry muttered. "This feels really gay."

"Look on the bright side," I said. "At least you finally got to first base with somebody."

We proceeded like that, hand in hand, our pace glacially slow, until—"I think I see a light up ahead," Henry said.

He was right. There was illumination, very faint, coming from up ahead of us. We continued, and I realized that as we approached it, the utter blackness to either side of me became shadows, then a haze of gray . . .

The basement was some sort of storage area, I intuited, for all sorts of factory implements I couldn't begin to fathom the nature of. My brain couldn't help but conceive of them as torture implements, though, and I shuddered. Fortunately, though, they remained on either side of us, and we had a clear, concrete path in front of our feet. We passed a bank of lockers on our right—for employees? I wondered—then a cluster of mop buckets and dirty mops clustered around a sink that gleamed white amidst the gloom.

We continued toward the light. At length, we drew up on the periphery of it. Hanging from the ceiling, one bare light bulb cast a circle of light outward in a radius of about ten feet from a bare concrete wall. The light bulb illuminated—

—*oh holy mother of God,* I thought—

—a scene straight out of nightmares. Either that, or a really, really kinky porno. A bukkake ring of at least a dozen of the dog-headed monstrosities encircled Fister and Victoria, who were bound together back to back, in the center. All the dog-headed demons were naked—and they were apparently human enough from the neck down—and stroking their members.

And apparently, even canine demons needed a little erotic assistance, for there was a large flat-screen TV plugged into the wall facing away from Henry and me that blared out a soundtrack that sounded like the deflowering of various barnyard animals.

Thankfully, none of the demons were paying any attention to their surroundings. Henry and I veered off and dove for cover behind a stray metal bin before any of the creatures could see us. We struggled in concert to bring our breathing, which was threatening hyperventilation, under control, and finally when we'd somewhat mastered our own terror, we both pivoted, pulled ourselves up with our fingertips on the lip of the aluminum bin, and peered over the top.

Fister and Victoria may have been bound back to back with a pair of ropes, but the demons had apparently forgotten to gag them. Their mistake. Fister was doing his level best to forestall the demons' inevitable ejaculations. "Looking a little saggy there, kemosabe," he said to one of the demons around the circle. "That's okay, don't take it too hard. Happens to everybody when they get to be your age." He shifted his address to another of the creatures. "Whoa, dude, now that's a cock only a mother could love." And then, to another: "I guess Elvis was right . . . you surely ain't never caught a rabbit with that thing."

Victoria caught on to the ploy, too. She squinted theatrically at one of the demons. "Is it up yet, snookums? 'Cause I can't really tell without my glasses." Then, to another: "And what are you supposed to be, sweetie? A Chihuahua?"

The taunting was having the desired effect. Several of the demons were studiously avoiding looking at Fister or Victoria, concentrating instead on the bizarre porno playing on the TV screen, and several more still were vigorously beating their meat, a clear sign of tumescence inhibition if ever there was one.

"What do we do?" Henry whispered to me. "What do you think is gonna happen when—"

"When their cocks start going off?" I finished for him. "I'm guessing those things didn't get their dog heads by accident."

Henry's eyes went wide. "They're not turning my mom into one of them. She's enough of a b-b-female dog already."

He made to rush off into the bukkake circle, but I caught him first and steered him back down into our hiding place behind the bin. "Are you crazy?" I snapped. "You can't go rushing headlong into a bukkake circle with a dozen demons." I pointed to my eye, which was blazing away beneath my shades. "C'mon, Morpheus, you know what demon jizz can do to you. We need a plan. Some sort of diversion."

"Great," he said, "one of us is the diversion . . . so what does the other one do?"

"Well . . ." *Good question*, I thought. How exactly were we going to distract all twelve members of the bukkake circle and lead them away from Fister and Victoria? We couldn't very well lead them on a merry chase through the basement, not without being able to see where we were going only a few feet from the one bare swinging light bulb . . .

And we were running out of time. Fister and Victoria were doing their level best to forestall the inevitable, but there were a dozen captors. And at that moment, one of the canine hybrid demons was already pumping furiously and breathing spasmodically in the universal harbinger of the money shot. And a second later, he stepped forward from the circle and knelt down to get a good aim at Victoria's and Fister's faces.

I shot Henry a quick look. "So much for plans," I said. "They're overrated anyway, right?" I broke from behind our hiding spot, bellowed an ear-splitting "*Nooooooooooo!*", and charged directly into the center of the bukkake circle, pushing two of the dog faced demons out of my way and dove protectively in front of Fister and Victoria.

Just as the creature's cannon went off. I felt something wet against my cheek, but I ignored it. I flung my arms protectively around Victoria and Fister, serving as a human shield. The creature hissed at me as it shot one, two more wads, and then finished. But instead of reaching out to attack me, it stumbled backward, back toward its spot next to its brethren in the bukkake ring, as if repelled by some invisible barrier.

I drew back a bit from Fister and Victoria. "Are you guys okay?" I asked. "You didn't . . . ahm . . . get any on you, did you?"

"Mikey!" Fister cried. "I knew you'd make it!" He paused. "You are Mikey, aren't you?"

"Who the hell else would I be?"

"Oh, no one. God, am I glad to see you."

It was all the happy reunion we were going to have time for. There was still the matter of the dozen self-spanking dogs surrounding us. Slowly, I got to my feet, and turned to face the creatures.

It was then that I noticed that the collar of my shirt was smoking furiously where a gobbet of the cur's jizz had landed. But the load on my cheek merely felt . . . wet. No burning sensation, no pain of having my entire face completely re-written by the power of the demon's seed. I wiped it off with the back of my hand.

The Macarena Incantatem, I realized. I reminded myself to write a thank-you note to the Wyrd Sisters if I ever made it out of here alive. That spell was totally badass.

And it was apparently the only thing keeping the canines from attacking me. Not that they didn't try: a couple of them surged forward, but yelped and recoiled, their noses wrinkling in disgust, as if confronting an invisible barrier.

Emboldened, I spread both my hands in the universal gesture of *bring it*. "That's right, bitches," I said. "This territory's already been marked."

They snarled and bared their teeth, but they kept their positions around the circle and came no closer. I took advantage and started to worry at the ropes binding Fister's and Victoria's hands.

"You figured out my text, I see," Fister said. "You found the coven?"

"Yeah."

"What about Henry?" Victoria whispered. "Please tell me he's safe. You didn't bring him here, did you?"

"Well . . . I—"

Damn, those fucking things had really tied those bonds tight. This was going to take a while. Did we even have a while? Who knew just exactly how long the *Macarena Incantatem* would keep these things at bay? We were still surrounded, after all. A perfect little standoff.

And the demons knew it. "You'll never escape," one of them, a gray-furred schnauzer-looking one grunted at us. His voice was gravelly, like a human's, but his words came out in clipped little barking jerks, like an aggressive vocal ejaculation.

"Oh yeah?" I taunted it, trying to sound far more confident than I actually felt. "What are you gonna do about it, huh?" For good measure I faked a lunge at him, and was relieved when it made him and both the mutts on either side of him backpedal a step in reaction.

The schnauzer pointed to one of his brethren across the circle. "We may not be able to penetrate your . . ." he scowled, "*protections*, but our human minions will have no such problem."

I followed the line of his outstretched finger. One of his brethren had fished a cell phone out of his pocket and was mumbling something I couldn't quite make out into it.

Human minions. Fuck it all! I thought. He must be referring to all the guys we'd heard boning each other in the various offices of the factory. "Oh yeah?" I said, but my voice cracked, and my bravado was melting away by the second. "They were a little busy with each other the last time I checked." How long ago had that been? Too long, I realized. As near to climax as some of the pairings had sounded, we were bound to have company—

"Just hold it right there," a stereotypically effeminate voice trying to sound butch said.

—right about now. My heart sank. And we'd been doing so well.

A pair of men wearing Dockers and untucked, hastily-buttoned shirts emerged into the pale light cast by the lone light bulb. One of them was holding a gun trained on Henry, who walked in front with his hands in the air. "I believe this little fellow belongs to you?"

Henry trotted over to join us. The canines hissed and melted out of his way as he passed. They fanned out and formed two lines on either side of us, while the two men stood between the two lines, boxing us in. The one on the left trained his pistol on us.

"Henry!" Victoria called.

"Mom!"

Victoria's hands were still bound behind her back, so she couldn't quite throw her arms around her son, so Henry dutifully knelt down beside her as they enjoyed their brief little reunion.

"Henry, what on earth are you doing here . . . you should be . . . oh my god, you stink."

"Nice to see you, too, mom." Henry muttered.

"Aw, how touching," the man with the gun said. His companion cupped his hands to his heart and batted his eyelashes in a prissy mocking gesture. At that moment they were joined by four more men, none of them dogs (though not exactly prizes, either). They'd come in a hurry; two of them were tucking in their shirts as they trotted into the light.

"What do we have here?" one of them asked. He was a short, middle-aged man with jowls that made him look similar to the boxer demon standing to his right. "Intruders? How on earth did you get this far?"

"You . . . uh . . . were kind of busy when we walked by," I said.

Another two men, late to the party, trotted up— one of them had forgotten to button his fly—which made us penned in by a dozen dog demons and eight human gays, by my count. *Shit.*

The jowly man addressed himself to the leader of the demons. "What would you have us do with them, o blessed one?" he asked.

"'Blessed one?'" Henry piped up. "You do know they're total dogs, right?"

"Silence!" the jowly man cried. "You, young man, should not mock the angels of the lord."

"'Angels of the lord?'" Henry looked from the line of dogs on the right, to the one on the left, then back to the line of humans. "You do know they're dogs, right? I mean, come on. What kind of angels of the lord are supposed to look like Boston Terriers? I mean, you've gotta be able to see that, right?"

Nearly in unison, the eight human men gasped and clutched their hands to their hearts. The one who had spoken made the sign of the cross, and then the remaining five followed suit like good little sheep. Then, the one who had spoken, whom I guessed was the leader—my mind deemed him "the spokesgay"— held up both hands in front of him palms outward like a televangelist, closed his eyes, and intoned, "We are of God; he that knoweth God heareth us; he that is not of God heareth not us. Hereby we know the Spirit of truth, and the spirit of error."

"Amen!" his fellow humans intoned. And then they made a show of falling to their knees in obeisance to the line of doggy demons on their left, and then repeated the gesture to the ones on the right.

The schnauzer, the leader of the demons, magnanimously sketched a sign of benison to the men, who beamed and received his blessing as if *they* were the lapdogs who'd just been patted on the head by their master.

Henry had watched this scene with just about as much incredulity as I had. "So . . . I'm guessing that's a no?" he said.

The spokesgay scowled. "I wouldn't expect heathens to recognize the messengers of the lord," he said.

"So just for the sake of argument," I cut in, "say they are angels. Don't tell me you're devout Catholic gays. That's just . . . doesn't compute."

The spokesgay bristled. "We're not *gay!*" he said. He drew out the last word to at least twice its normal length to give it an extra special weight of heinousness.

"Um, okay, so maybe you don't like labels. 'Bi-sexual', maybe? 'Bi-curious?' 'Flexibly amorous?' Am I getting warmer here?"

"The Lord sent his angels to us to cure us of all impure impulses. We have renounced our former lives of sin and wickedness."

"Bloody hell," Fister muttered. "Ex-gays. No wonder it smells like sanctimonious bullshit in here."

"Ah," I said. "I see. Well, then, congratulations on renouncing all your sin and wickedness and shit. So how's that working out for you?"

"We have been washed clean by the blood of Christ!" the spokesgay exclaimed, and his brethren rejoindered with a hearty "*Amen!*"

I turned to the demons. "I think you all need to wash a little harder," I said.

"Silence!" the spokesgay cried, sounding like a petulant child. He waved the pistol at me. "Step away from those two now. And keep your hands up where I can see them."

"All right," I said. I did as he said, moving away from Fister and Victoria. I held both my hands up in the air. "So let's say for the sake of argument that these angels of the lord are helping you to repress your homosexual tendencies. So what's with all the urinal cakes? How are those supposed to 'cure' all the rest of the gays in the world?"

The spokesgay grinned. "They have been blessed by the angels of the lord. They will restore righteousness to the entire world."

I frowned. "Urinal cakes? Really? The angels of the lord have taken to blessing urinal cakes now?"

"They already gloated about it to us," Fister cut in. "Whatever you do, don't make me sit through the fucking holier-than-thou rhetoric again. Here, Mikey, let me catch you guys up to speed. The urinal cakes contain inert demon spores. Once they're activated, the spores will travel through men's urinary streams and take root in their urethras and wreak changes in men's sperm so that no more gays will ever be born."

"What?" I turned to the jowly spokesgay. "I'll grant you the spores, and the delivery system is ingenious, but you can't seriously believe that spores could actually only target gay men. Don't tell me you actually believed that explanation? That's the shittiest science I've ever heard."

"*Science!*" the spokesgay scoffed. "What need have we of science when we have the grace of the angels of the lord?"

I shook my head. "Did you ever bother to think what the angels of the lord would need with a bunch of tainted urinal cakes? I mean, why couldn't they just wave their arms and make the entire world straight again?"

"Uh—" The spokesgay's face creased as he puzzled over my question for a second. But then his countenance rapidly cleared as he came up with the answer: "The Lord works in mysterious ways," he said.

"Uh-huh. Of course he does." I turned to the schnauzer demon. "The urinal cakes really are tainted with demon spores, aren't they?" I asked.

"We prefer the term 'blessed,' but basically, yes."

"But I'm guessing these spores don't just target gay men, do they?"

The schnauzer laughed, and his cronies followed suit, and their laughter rang out like the maniacal barking of a pack of dogs chasing after a squirrel. "Congratulations," the schnauzer said. "You're certainly much smarter than this bunch of faggots."

The spokesgay's and his brethren's jaws all dropped open wide at the schnauzer's blunt words. "Master ? I—I don't understand—"

"Oh, put a dick in it, will you, Eugene?" the schnauzer snapped. He strode forward to stand in front of the man he'd named Eugene, and his posture was all arrogance and gloating. Now all eight of the ex-gays traded confused looks; as a unit, they frowned and gaped at the schnauzer, as if they hadn't heard correctly. Ignoring Eugene, who visibly wilted and looked to his cronies at the "angels'" sudden turn, the schnauzer focused his attention on me. "These prissy little queens would do anything to believe that there's a cure for their own natures. And do you know the beautiful thing: there is." He grinned, which made his mouth open wide and his pink tongue loll out. "Us."

"You? You mean . . ." I did the math. I felt a little slow on the uptake, but eventually the dots connected in my head. "*That's* what the spores do," I said. "They corrupt men's sperm—"

"So the entire next generation of children born in this world will be *our* children. So that demonkind will inherit the earth!"

I considered the implications of his words. "That's . . . that's . . ." I fumbled for words. "That's so fucked up."

The schnauzer grinned again. "We owe you a debt of gratitude," he said.

"What . . . us?" I said. "We're not here to help you . . ."

"Of course not. But you've helped us to accelerate our plans. The shipments of urinal cakes have been progressing for months. Already men all over the world carry our spores in their urethras."

"You mean—"

"All we've lacked is a power source powerful enough to cast the spell to activate all the spores at once."

"A power source? What the hell powers an incantation of that magnitude?"

The schnauzer smirked. "The soul of a virgin should suffice. And here you've brought us one as a gift."

"What?" Victoria shrieked. Her hands were still tied behind her back, but she struggled to her feet and cut in front of me to glare her fury at the schnauzer. "You cocksucking motherfucking bitches, you leave my son alone!"

The schnauzer guffawed. "Your son? Oh, good lord, no. His aura's about as virginal as a common back-alley whore."

The blaze of Victoria's fury cooled somewhat. "Wha?—I don't understand." She turned to her son. "Henry?"

Henry spread his arms innocently. "Chill, ma, it was just a handjob."

The schnauzer *tsked* theatrically. He held up his clawed right index finger and waved it reprovingly at Henry. "Lots of hand jobs, if I'm reading your aura correctly, young man. So much seed spilled by the hands of others. Adolescent experimentation besmirches so many otherwise pure souls."

"Oh," Victoria said, relieved. "You mean his little classmates he invites over for sleepovers. Of course I know about that."

"*Ma*!" Henry protested.

I frowned. "Wait a minute . . . if not Henry . . ." Who the hell else here qualified as even more virginal than Henry? Fister . . . I could rule that one out. I'd been in the front seat while he'd popped his cherry to Janet Leister in my back seat. Victoria? The mere existence of Henry precluded that. And me . . . well, I wasn't exactly a semen-spewing stud-muffin, but I was no fresh unspoiled snowfall, either. I could at least boast more than a handjob on my sexual resume. "Who—?"

The schnauzer stepped forward. "The one you carry inside you," he said. He waved a hand in front of my face—

—and a wave of fatigue rolled over me. Unable to stop myself, I yawned. I tried to open my mouth to protest, to demand to know what was happening to me, but all my words came out as nothing more than an incoherent yawn.

I surrendered to sleep.

Part Three

Dick

CHAPTER FIVE

Sweet, sweet dreams—dreams of warmth and wetness, like floating in a golden womb (a gestation the circumstances of my own demonic birth could only render inside the book and volume of my imagination)—vanished into the ether amidst the violence of a rude, rude awakening.

I tried to blink the fog of sleep away. *Too soon,* I intuited. Normally I relished the return to consciousness after an entire day banished to the recesses of my host's mind, and I welcomed it with open arms like Fräulein Maria greeting the hills that were alive with the sound of music. But this time was different. This time I was a grumpy slugabed whose covers were pulled off him far too soon.

I blinked. My perception was slow to focus, but the first thing I perceived was a sound: *barking.* And lots of it. But this was no random barking of hounds as if a squirrel had been placed in plain view of the humane society kennels; rather, it was structured, rhythmic . . . like chanting.

And when I blinked the sleep out of my eyes and my vision cohered, I realized why. First I beheld a line of eight rather plain-looking men ranging from their mid-thirties to early middle age. One of them held a gun trained on me—

—and on Fister, Victoria, and Henry, I realized. We were all standing together. Or rather, Henry and I were standing, and Fister and Victoria were on the bare concrete floor, their hands bound in front of them. "Dick!" Henry called by way of greeting.

It was a rather muted greeting. "What the hell have you guys been up to while I was asleep?" I responded.

It was a rhetorical question. My gaze was drawn away from them, to my left, where an entire row of humanoid creatures with the heads of dogs was emitting a guttural stream of barks. Demons were easy enough to recognize: they were like me— denizens of some other plane—but so unlike me at the same time. I recognized their barking for what it was: the intonation of some incantation in their own language.

I swiveled my gaze to the right, and there beheld yet another row of dog-headed creatures engaged in the same occupation. And then I glanced over my shoulder to see that there was a wall behind us, with a large-screen TV in the corner that was screening some really, really kinky porno involving a bevy or barnyard animals. Normally my attention might have lingered longer on the porno, but I was suddenly far more concerned with my own situation—*our* situation, really, the gang and I—and just how fucked we were: backs against the wall, demons on the left and the right, and really effete-looking stoolies in front, one of them with a gun trained on us.

And just then, the dogs' barking chant intensified. I looked to the right, and saw that one of the dog demons was holding something in his outstretched right hand. I stared at it, and frowned. What the hell was it? It was pink, and puck-shaped, and smelled somewhat disinfectant-y to my heightened sense of smell . . .

A urinal cake.

I experienced a sensation of tugging. Not *physical* tugging at the body I shared with my host, but rather, a sensation of something tugging at my entire being—my consciousness, if you will. My consciousness was being pulled toward the urinal cake by the power of the demons' incantation. *Into* the urinal cake, I clarified to myself, for I perceived a whirling vortex that encompassed the surface of the disc, its own little miniature gateway to another plane of existence. And little by little, the essence of *me* was being sucked across the threshold into the event horizon.

I quickly accessed my host's memories in an attempt to comprehend the situation I'd awoken in. And I realized: the mystical power of my virgin being was being sacrificed to power the diabolical network of the demons' urinal cakes. This brief, tragic life I'd been born into . . . it was so unfair. I was but a newborn babe in the grand scheme of things, but even a normal newborn babe had had more sexual gratification than I; at least a newborn babe got to suck on its mother's nipples. That was so much more than I could boast.

I groaned and swayed precariously as the energies draining away from me threatened my balance. It seemed I was going to cease to exist before I'd experienced hardly anything of this brave new world. *Dammit*, I thought. If I'd known this was going to happen, I'd have gone ahead and popped my cherry last night at Rub-a-Dub's.

Popped my cherry . . .

Of course! That was the only way to change the equation of this situation. The demons' power source demanded the mystical energies of a virgin. And Henry was disqualified because of a mere handjob. Which meant—

I focused my attention on the gay with the gun. His aim was soft, and in fact, he was standing looking rather superfluous, wondering how this situation had spiraled so out of his control, as were all his gay cronies. "You," I said. My voice came out as little more than a plaintive croak.

He spread his hands helplessly. "We never meant for this to happen!" he cried, his voice high-pitched. "All we wanted was for the gayness to end. We never meant . . . we didn't mean it! You've gotta believe me."

"Blow me," I said.

"It—it . . . they deceived us. The devil can take a pleasing shape . . . it wasn't our fault. We just—"

"No," I gritted out. Words were coming harder as more and more of my being was sucked across into the disc of the one urinal cake to rule them all. "I mean . . . will you just . . . shut up . . . and blow me?"

I struggled mightily to reach down, fumble with the zipper on my pants, pull it down, and free my willie.

He was painfully stupid, but even he understood the message inherent in an unzipped fly and a pecker dangling invitingly before his eyes. He crossed the few steps separating us, knelt down in front of me, and went down on me. And with my cock in his mouth, he completely lost interest in the gun in his hand. Henry stepped up and deftly took it out of his hand. Committed as he was to my cock, Eugene hardly seemed to notice.

The demons hissed with annoyance as they realized what I was up to. Their lines tried to step forward to stop Eugene, but Henry grasped my plan straight away; he planted his *Macarena Incantatemed* ass in front of me to act as my shield, and the demons were stymied once again by the protection of the *Macarena Incantatem*.

Sweet holy Jesus, Eugene was a pro. He'd obviously had lots of practice. He grasped the base of my shaft with his hand and deep-throated the whole thing with a notable lack of any gag reflex whatsoever. Suddenly the direness of the situation in the factory basement receded in the face of that sweet, wet pair of lips on my shaft. Eugene licked, and teased, and jiggled my balls for that little extra flourish—

"You're too late!" the schnauzer cried. He cackled maniacally. "His soul belongs to us!"

Second by second, the demons' spell was also nearer to its own climax. And as more and more of my own life essence was tugged into the vortex of the urinal cake, the sensations of Eugene's hummer receded. Inch by inch, synapse by synapse, I was losing the connection with my host's body and all the attendant sensations of the flesh. Eugene and I were now in a race with the dogs to see who could finish first.

No pressure. The entire fate of humanity rested on my ability to blow my load.

Don't think about that, I admonished myself. *Just relax into it. Think about all the things that make you horny . . .*

Which wasn't too hard. I was born horny, after all. I was a member of the race of the horniest creatures in existence. I was born to be horny. Horniness was my superpower.

So I closed my eyes and found my zen: rock-hard boners and moist, dripping crannies, pearl necklaces and the tang of spunk on the tip of the tongue, hummers and quickies and back-alley gangbangs, booby licking and backdoor banditry, jug squirting and muff munching and MILF diving, twink juices and twincest and bondage and bedrooms, foreplay and fucking and fellatio, naughty nurses and stiff-pricked policemen and public humiliation, dildos and anal beads and fatty fold fucking, golden showers and plating and foot fetishes . . . all the brilliant flavors of the sexual panoply, all the things I'd dreamed of and watched on my host's computer screen and hoped to one day experience for myself. . . the beautiful, exquisite humanity of slapping skin against skin in all its infinite variations . . . and yes, even plain old vanilla missionary—I considered it all, like I really was Fräulein Maria and these were just a few of my favorite things.

And my consciousness's tenuous connection to the flesh of my host, drained away almost to nothing, came rushing back in full force as I crossed over the edge, that mystical and insanely powerful moment between buildup and climax, wherein the big glorious O went from a consummation devoutly to be wished to an utter inevitability like the tide crashing against the shore.

I pushed Eugene's head to the side and pumped myself the rest of the way home.   My urethra spasmed, and the first sticky gobbets of sweet release fired forth from the fertile loins of my cannon, arcing up and into the air. Any ordinary money shot might have sailed a few feet at best only to splatter like an ill-fated Rohrschach blot on the bare concrete floor; but this one was destined for greater things. It was caught up in the arc of the demons' spell which was sucking my consciousness into the vortex of the one urinal cake to rule them all. My jizz slammed into the open vortex—

—and the dozen doggy demons shrieked in rage and fury, even though they were powerless to stop it—

—and then another spurt, and another, and yet another arced across and into the gaping chasm the width of the urinal cake. The cake in the head demon's hand soaked up my spunk hungrily, like a guzzling mouth with a hunger all its own . . .

. . . and then the vortex flashed once, twice, and blinked out, leaving nothing but an ordinary, inert pink disinfectant-y disk. And at the same time the demons' incantation sputtered and died, releasing its hold on my consciousness. I slammed back into my body—well, it was my host's body, but I was firmly in the driver's seat now—and I felt the glorious rush of all the attendant perceptions of a body that had just blown its load: the residual post-orgasmic throb from the balls, the sensation of thrumming that seemingly permeated every nerve ending . . .

It was a beautiful moment, but unfortunately, spoiled all too quickly by the hellish howling of the demons. They shrieked out their demonic fury at the failure of their incantation and being denied the incarnation of their species on earth. They gnashed their canine teeth together and growled at us, but the iron-clad protection of the *Macarena Incantatem* held them back.

Henry helped Fister and Victoria to their feet. Their hands were still tied, but their feet were free. The three of them came forward to stand next to me. "Dick," Fister said, "that was awesome."

Victoria smiled down at my slowly deflating boner. "Now that's a totally epic way to pop your cherry. Way to go, stud."

Henry clapped me on the shoulder. "That was righteous, Dick." He glared defiantly at the line of demons. "Take that, you b-b-b-oh, darnit."

"What are we going to do about them?" Fister asked, indicating the demons. "We can't just—"

"Leave them to us," Eugene said. He strode forward and held out his hand to Henry for the gun that Henry held in his hand. Henry considered for a moment, and then handed it over.

Eugene crossed in front of us and trained the weapon on the line of demons. "*You*," he said, "you tricked us, you *bitches*." He spat this last word like it was poisoned. "You'll pay. Oh, lordie lordie, yes, you'll pay."

"Well. I guess our job here is finished." I looked to Fister, Victoria, and Henry, and I smiled. They returned the smile, and it made my heart glad to see the acceptance in their eyes. All it had taken was nearly losing my soul.

And that revelation was perhaps the best thing of all: even I had a soul. The dogs had confirmed it by choosing me to activate their spell. *The soul of a virgin*.

Well . . . not so much anymore. But that was okay. I had plenty more cherries to pop.

Epilogue

Mikey

EPILOGUE

"So," I said when I had Fister, Victoria, and Henry all assembled around my kitchen table, "you mean I've had Dick inside me all this time?"

Henry failed to contain a snicker, and his mother offhandedly reached out and smacked the backside of his head. Fister grinned his idiotic schoolboy, grin, too. "Yeah," he said. "Ever since that day I hosted an Angrafilic eritifal in my body and I accidentally jizzed in your eye." He reached over and clapped me on the shoulder. "Look at it this way, though. Dick lives in your consciousness, and I'm the one who knocked you up, so I guess that makes us kind of like gay dads."

"And you never told me?"

"Well, we only just found out about Dick last night," Victoria said. "We debated whether or not we should tell you, but we all decided we'd better wait. I mean, you can be a bit of a bitch about these things, you know. No offense."

I shrugged. She kind of had a point. In fact, the whole idea of Dick was kind of weirding me out even now.

"You'd really like Dick if you could meet him," Henry said. "He's a real stand-up kind of guy." He beamed. "See what I did there?"

I ignored his jape. "Do you think . . . is that even possible? Could we ever meet?"

"Who knows?" Fister spread his hands. "You could talk to him, though. He was born inside your consciousness, not the other way around. Now that you know he's there, I guess you could like . . . I don't know, communicate somehow. Leave messages for each other, or some shit like that. Work out a system."

I sighed. It was a little disconcerting to know that every time I went to sleep I would have to surrender my body to someone else. There were two tenants in residence inside my body now. Like it or not, I had a roommate. At least, from what Fister, Victoria, and Henry had told me of the events that had transpired both last night at Rub-a-Dub's and earlier today in the factory, my body seemed to be in good hands . . . when it was out of my hands, that was. Still, it would take some getting used to.

"Look on the bright side," Fister said. "Today, you, Dick, and your dick saved the world."

I sighed. There was that, at least. "Do you think we're safe now?" I asked. "I mean, I can't help thinking of all those urinal cakes they shipped with demon spores. I'm not sure I can ever pee in a urinal again."

"They're dormant," Fister said. "They never managed to finish the spell to activate the network. Pissing on a urinal cake should be as safe as . . ." He trailed off as he floundered for a good analogy.

"As pi-pi-peeing on someone's face," Henry said. Then, he scowled at his own traitorous mouth. "Drat."

"What about Henry?" I asked Fister and Victoria. "Do you think . . . will the effects of the *Macarena Incantatem* wear off?"

"Who knows?" Victoria shrugged. "Though so far, I kind of like it." She ruffled her son's hair. "To be honest, I think it's a bit of an improvement."

Henry glared at her, but any retort he might have made would probably have been hamstrung by the *Macarena Incantatem* anyway. "It's a really powerful spell," he said instead. "There may still be other effects yet to come."

"Well, that's cheering," I said. "As if sharing my body with Dick weren't enough change to get used to—" I stopped at Henry's poor attempt to restrain a guffaw, and I shook my head. "Couldn't we at least give him a better name?" I looked to Fister. "We are his parents, after all."

"Oh, come on, doc," Henry said. "He named himself Dick. Besides, what's in a name?" Henry grinned. "A Dick by any other name would smell as sweet."

I looked to him, impressed. "You've been brushing up your Shakespeare."

He shrugged. "I pay attention in English class sometimes."

"Well, then." I got up from the table, and stretched. "I know it's still early, but I'm beat, and I've got a killer headache. Sharing your head with someone else will do that to you, I guess. If you don't mind, I think I'm going to my well-deservèd bed."

"By all means," Fister said. "Don't worry. We'll show ourselves out."

I didn't believe him, but it didn't matter. I left them there at my kitchen table and retreated to my bedroom. I considered flopping straight away onto my bed, but instead I detoured to my bathroom, and stood in front of the mirror. I didn't look any different, not in any way I could tell, but knowing you were wanking for two from now on sure did change your perspective in all kinds of unexpected ways.

And one thing was for certain: I was horny. "Down, Dick," I muttered. "Down, boy."

It didn't help. *Well*, I thought, *I guess I could rub one out before going to bed . . .*

AUTHOR'S AFTERWARD

My dearest sick fucks,

I hereby express my extreme gratitude to you for taking a third whack at this with me (errr . . . you know what I mean). Offending people with the *Psycho Proctologists* has turned into more fun than I ever could have thought when I spewed the words of the first book onto the page, and it's gratifying to know that there are people out there sick enough to go along for the ride. I very much have appreciated hearing from those who dropped me a line on the first two books, so if you've got a spare moment, consider emailing me at psychoproctologists@hotmail.com. Kudos, accolades, disapproval, moral outrage . . . it's all welcome. Especially the moral outrage. 'Cause that's the nectar that nourishes my sick, sad, sadistic fucked-up soul. That, and the pathetic, incoherent ramblings of Pat Robertson. Man, you just can't make that shit up.

You can also visit my YouTube channel, where you can see homemade book trailers:

www.youtube.com/psychoproctologists

Or on Facebook:

www.facebook.com/psychoproctologists

Or drop by the Psycho Proctologists blog and leave a comment:

www.psychoproctologists.blogspot.com

Sincerely,

W.W. Pecker